S0-ABC-868

The Haunted Shul
and other
Devora Doresh Mysteries

by

Carol Korb Hubner

illustrated by

Devorah Kramer

Judaica Press • 1981
New York

Copyright © 1979
by
Carol Korb Hubner

Revised Second Edition
Copyright © 1981
by
The Judaica Press, Inc.
New York, N.Y.

All Rights Reserved,
including the right of reproduction in whole or in part,
in any form

ISBN 0-910818-14-2

This book is dedicated to
Leah Miriam, Sarah
Moshe and Yitzchak Aharon

MANUFACTURED IN THE UNITED STATES OF AMERICA

Contents

The Missing Papers

evora! Devora!"

Devora Doresh heard her friend calling her from the street. She got up from her desk and walked over to the window, which was wide open to greet the beautiful spring day.

"All right, Kaila!" she called. "I'll be down in a few minutes." She returned to her desk, opened the drawer, and took out a pack of index cards. She checked to make sure her room was neat, then smiled to herself, flung a pink sweater around her shoulders and stepped across the hall into the kitchen.

Her mother was sitting at the kitchen table, looking over her guest list for the *melave malke** she had arranged for the *shul* sisterhood.

"I'm going out with Kaila, Mother," Devora reported. "I still have lots more index cards to give out."

Mrs. Doresh nodded. "Just be careful, Devora. Watch out for the things that might get lost and the things that have to be found."

Devora gave her mother a quick smile. When she had first told her parents about her idea of setting up a "Lost and Found" bureau, they had been quick to approve. *Rebbe* Doresh—as everyone called her father—

*"Farewell to the Sabbath Queen." This is a party given after the Sabbath with singing and refreshments as a farewell to the Day of Rest.

encouraged his daughter in all her many projects. Devora was considered one of the brightest girls in her class at Yocheved High School. But besides being a fine student, she was known for her readiness to help others. Even her one-girl "Lost and Found" bureau had been the result of her eagerness to be helpful. She had already helped many families in her neighborhood find things they had lost—some of them quite valuable. As a matter of fact, Devora was fast becoming known as a detective; grown-ups had begun to call her to solve problems they considered as mysteries. When people asked her how she was able to find the answers to so many questions, she told them it was all thanks to her Torah studies at Yocheved.

"With a last name like Doresh," said her younger brother Chaim, who had just turned 8, "what else could my sister do?" Doresh happens to be the Hebrew word for "investigator."

Kaila was outside eagerly waiting for her friend. Chaim was standing under a tree nearby, reading aloud from one of Devora's typed index cards.

"Devora Doresh
Lost and Found Bureau
Will help you find anything you lose
612 East Mapleton
Phone: 991–3340"

He made a face. "So tell me, Kaila," he asked his sister's friend. "If I lose my ball, is she going to run and find it for me?" Without waiting for Kaila's reply, he threw his red ball into the air and caught it as it came down. "Nope!" he decided out loud. "Takes too much time." He threw his ball into the air again and caught it moments before it fell to the ground. Then, with a nod to Kaila, he walked off, tossing his ball from one hand to the other.

Meanwhile, Devora was running down the stairs. She pushed open the door of her house and stepped out into the street.

All the houses on East Mapleton looked pretty much alike. Some of the houses had chicken-wire gates; others had fences of wrought iron or painted wood. A few of the houses had bay windows instead of the large square picture windows of the others. But otherwise they were all the same: two-family houses with the owner living in the upstairs apartment and the tenant on the ground floor below. An indoor stairway of fifteen steps led from the landlord's apartment to the foyer of the ground floor. "You'll never have to worry about icy steps in the winter," the build r of the houses would tell anyone interested in buying one of the homes.

Almost everyone in the neighborhood was Jewish, neither rich nor poor. The people were all friendly with each other. They sent their younger children to the same neighborhood yeshiva. Only the high schoolers had to travel to school by subway or bus. "Hi, Kaila," said Devora as she closed the outer door of her house. "I've typed up some more cards to give out."

"Forget the cards, Devora," said Kaila, with a wave of her hand. "I have some serious business for you. A new case, *Gemora Kop.*" Devora pursed her lips and looked at her friend. *Gemora Kop* was the nickname Devora's Hebrew teacher, *Morah* Hartman, had given her star pupil. A *Gemora Kop* is a student of the Talmud who has the special gift of reasoning needed to follow the thinking of the Sages. *Morah* Hartman felt that Devora had this ability, and the name stuck, particularly when Devora was about to start work on a new "case."

"Mr. Goldberg came home from his office for an early lunch," Kaila reported excitedly. "He lives on 543 East Mapleton, you know. There must have been some burglars in the house, and he caught them red-handed. But one of them had a gun and shot Mr. Goldberg. He's in the hospital now, unconscious."

Devora blinked. "That's terrible! How did you find out?"

"I saw the police car in front of their house. I asked all sorts of questions because I figured you would want to know."

Devora shook her head. "Why would I want to know?"

"You might want to help search for the missing papers."

"What missing papers? What are you talking about?"

Kaila started to tell all she knew.

"Mr. Goldberg had some very important papers—certificates, Mrs. Goldberg said—hidden somewhere in his house. Nobody knows where these certificates are hidden. All we know is that when the Goldbergs moved into the house six months ago, Mr. Goldberg had the builder make a secret compartment somewhere in his apartment for his important papers and jewels. He's in the jewelry business, and he wanted to be safe. Of course he told Mrs. Goldberg where the compartment is, but right now she's so upset that the doctor gave her some pills and she can't remember anything and the builder is out of the country. The trouble is that she has to turn over these papers to the bank no later than next week. If she doesn't find them until then, the Goldbergs will lose a lot of money."

The two girls walked over to the Goldbergs' house. The outside door was wide open. Chaim Doresh was standing in the archway bouncing his ball against the Goldbergs' steps. He was singing, "A,B,C,D,E,F,G" to his own little tune:

"A,B,C,D,E,F,G,
H,I,J,K,L,M,N,O,P.
Devora Doresh Gemora Kop,
Won't you tell us what is up?
When you solve this mystery,
Think how famous you will be."

He hit his ball hard against the last step of the house, and the ball flew over his head as he sang out the letter "P" again.

Devora rang the Goldberg bell. Mrs. Goldberg opened the door. Her face was very pale and her lips were trembling.

"Yes?" she asked in a low voice.

"Is there anything we can do to help?" Devorah asked gently.

"I'm afraid there isn't much you can do just now," Mrs. Goldberg replied. She put a handkerchief to her face and began to cry quietly.

A police officer stepped out from behind Mrs. Goldberg. It was Sergeant O'Malley from the neighborhood precinct.

"Girlie," he said, pointing his finger straight at Devora, "are you that Devora Doresh who opened up that 'Lost and Found' bureau? Well, why don't you just work at your 'Lost and Found' and keep out of things like this Goldberg business? This is a case for the police, not a game for little girls. The police will help find the thugs who shot Mr. Goldberg, and they'll also find the papers Mrs. Goldberg claims she lost."

Kaila hurried down the steps. She looked back at the tall, stern police sergeant and almost tripped over Devora who had already reached the bottom step.

"Oops, I'm sorry, Devora, but that sergeant scares me!"

The two girls stepped out into the street. Chaim was standing there, his ball in his hand. Beside him was an older boy, his friend Aryeh. "You heard the sergeant," said Aryeh. "Don't get mixed up in police business."

Kaila was almost crying. "But—we only wanted to know if we could help Mrs. Goldberg find her missing papers," she stammered, "and I know that Devora has

the best 'Lost and Found' bureau in the neighborhood."

Chaim laughed and bounced his ball on the ground. Again he began to bounce his ball against the Goldbergs' steps: One by one:

"A,B,C,D,E,F,G,

H,I,J,K,L,M,N,O,P . . ."

At the Yocheved High School the next day *Morah* Hartman, Devora's teacher, was reviewing with her class the story of how young David had fled from the anger of King Saul. David had hidden out in a cave. While he was hiding deep inside the cave, a spider had appeared and woven a thick web over the entrance to the cave. Moments later, King Saul arrived with his soldiers. Seeing the dense spider web across the mouth of the cave, he concluded that no one could have entered the cave recently and that David therefore had to be hiding out not there but in some other place. And so the king and his men had left, and David had been saved, and lived to become King of Israel. This experience, said *Morah* Hartman, had taught David an important lesson. Until that time he had often wondered of what possible good an ugly insect like the spider could be on earth. Now, at last, having been saved by the spider, he understood that every creature of G-d had its purpose. "And so, you can see," *Morah* Hartman continued, "that each and every creature on earth is important; none of them is too small to count in G-d's great plan."

That same afternoon, Devora heard a similar statement from *Reb* Dovid, who taught her class the writings of the Prophets. "There is not one letter in the Torah of G-d," he told the class, "that is not important. There is not one letter, not even a dot, in the Torah that is superfluous. Every letter is intended to tell us something. Every letter in the Torah has a message for those who seek to understand ... "

Every letter ... a message ...

A,B,C,D,E,F,G,

H,I,J,K,L,M,N,O,P ...

A thought flashed through Devora's mind but it went away before she had a chance to follow it further.

At home her mother told her that Mr. Goldberg was still unconscious, and that the lawyers were pressing Mrs. Goldberg for the certificates, telling her over and over again that if she did not remember where they were hidden, she would lose a great deal of money. At the supper table, the talk was all about the Goldbergs. The talk continued after Kaila arrived as usual to study the next day's lesson with Devora. The two girls worked well together and since they lived very near each other it was only natural that they should be study partners.

"You know, my parents were afraid to let me go out to come here tonight," Kaila said to *Rebbe* Doresh. "Ever since the burglary at the Goldbergs' house, they are scared somebody will attack me in the street."

Devora's father nodded his head. "As you put it, Kaila, we are only a few houses away from each other.

But if you were to break this distance down to the number of steps you have to walk from your house to ours, it would sound like a lot more—and all the more reason for your parents to be afraid. Just think of what could happen during the time you make all those steps."

"All those steps—plus fifteen," Chaim chimed in. "You mustn't forget the fifteen steps up to our house, you know. Every little bit counts."

Devora had been listening quietly to the conversation. Suddenly she remembered what *Morah* Hartman said that morning, and *Reb* Dovid that afternoon. "Everything was created with a purpose. Nothing in this world is superfluous. Not even one letter, one dot. . . . Every letter has a message for those who seek to understand . . ." Dots and letters. Without realizing it, she began to hum Chaim's tune:

"A,B,C,D,E,F,G,
H,I,J,K,L,M,N,O,P. . ."

As he sang out each letter, Chaim had bounced his ball against another step of the Goldberg's house. A,B,C. . . . How many letters? Why—sixteen! But each house on Mapleton had only fifteen steps. Or did—

"Is there anything wrong, Devora?" her mother asked.

Devora shook her head. "No, Mother. But I think I have the answer to Mrs. Goldberg's problem. May I be excused, please."

"Go ahead, dear. But please be careful," her mother said.

Devora went to her room to get her sweater and walked out of the house. She hummed Chaim's tune all the way to the Goldberg house:

"A,B,C,D,E,F,G,

H,I,J,K,L,M,N,O,P. . ."

Mrs. Goldberg answered the door. Sergeant O'Malley was still with her. He and his detail of policemen had been guarding the house for 24 hours.

"Mrs. Goldberg," Devora said, panting to catch her breath, "I think I know where your husband has his secret compartment!"

Mrs. Goldberg stared at Devora. Sergeant O'Malley gave her a long close look.

"Well, where is it?" they both asked together.

"You have one extra step," said Devora, pointing to the stairway. "All the other houses have fifteen steps; you have sixteen. I think that's the answer!"

Sergeant O'Malley carefully made his way down the steps, tapping each one gently with his wooden stick as he went. One of the steps gave off a hollow sound, different from the sound the wooden stick had made on all the others. Sergeant O'Malley bent over and began to feel around the step with his fingers.

"There it is, by golly!" he shouted." A button right in the step!" He pushed the button. The step opened up, revealing a locked drawer. "Where are your house keys, Mrs. Goldberg?" he asked.

The light of recall shone from Mrs. Goldberg's face and she no longer appeared tired. She ran up the steps and returned with a bunch of keys. She handed the keys to Sergeant O'Malley. Sure enough, one of the keys fitted the lock of the drawer. The drawer opened. Inside were folded papers held together with rubber bands.

"How on earth did you know about that extra step, Devora?" Sergeant O'Malley asked.

"From my school work," Devora quietly replied.

"Oh, come on," said the policeman. "Is that what they teach you in high school nowadays?"

"I'm serious," Devorah insisted. "Yesterday we learned at school that everything in the world was created with a purpose—even the letters in our books each are important in their own right. Yesterday when my little brother bounced his ball against each of your steps, he was singing the alphabet from the letter 'A' down to the letter 'P'. Now all the other houses on East Mapleton Street have fifteen steps. But 'P' is the sixteenth letter of the alphabet. So, you see—"

Sergeant O'Malley gave Devora an admiring look. But he was a policeman and was not used to praising high school girls for their intelligence. "As far as I'm concerned," he grunted, "an extra step just means another place for a spider to spin his web."

The Case of the Four Diamonds

n Shabbos morning almost everyone on East Mapleton Street could be found in the large synagogue at the corner of Adelaide Avenue. Devora Doresh and many of the other young people in the neighborhood especially admired the rabbi; they enjoyed listening to his sermons on the weekly Torah portion. Rabbi Shaya Epstein was no longer young, but his voice was still loud and clear, and though he had spent most of his life in Europe, his English was every bit as good as his Yiddish.

The Torah portion for that particular week dealt with a number of important events in the early history of the Jewish people. Rabbi Epstein summarized them in considerable detail, carefully explaining their meaning to us in the present day. First, there was the story of the twelve spies whom Moses had sent to Canaan in advance of the rest of the Children of Israel, and of the unforgivable sin these twelve men had committed by bringing back discouraging reports about the Land of Israel. Rabbi Epstein compared the men in that story to some of the people today who insist that parents should not allow their sons and daughters to settle in Israel because the country is constantly threatened by enemies.

Just as the twelve spies of old received their just punishment for their evil talk, said Rabbi Epstein, so, too, those who speak badly of Israel today will be put to shame.

The rabbi then turned to the commandment bidding every Jewish man to wear *tzitzith,* a four-cornered garment with fringes on each corner. The purpose of the fringes is to serve the Jew as reminders of all of G-d's other commandments so that he will not neglect any of them. This commandment is considered so important that even little boys of three and four already show off the *tzitzith* under their shirts and sweaters.

After services, Devora and her mother left the synagogue. In the street outside, Devora's father and her little brother were already waiting. Though Chaim was only 8 years old, he always sat quietly beside his father throughout the *davening** and almost never went outside in between to join the other boys for a few minutes of play in back of the Synagogue. The father, *Rebbe* Doresh, was an impressive-looking man, with a thin, long face, a long, pointed pitch-black beard, and big black eyes. His students at the yeshiva considered him a very strict teacher, but they liked and respected him, and many of them, along with their parents, turned to him for advice on problems of Jewish Law. Devora's mother, Mrs. Doresh, was a plump little woman with a fair complexion and a stylish blonde *sheitel.*** She was very active in the community, conducting classes for the

*Praying
**Wig

women on Shabbos and one other day each week. From time to time she substituted at the Yocheved High School when one of the teachers was absent.

That Shabbos afternoon, Devora and her friend Shira Hellman walked together to the *Oneg Shabbat* of their young girls' group. Blonde, blue-eyed Shira was always dressed in the latest teen-age fashions, but she never wore anything that was not *tzniyusdig*—modest and ladylike as befitted the Orthodox Jewish girl she was. Devora, too, wore only *tzniyusdig* dresses, not quite as fancy as Shira's, but she always looked crisp and neat. Perhaps her most striking features were her deep, dark eyes fringed by long, dark lashes.

Shira was excitedly telling Devora the news of her big sister's engagement. Officially, it was still supposed to be a secret, but everyone knew about it. Chana Hellman had spent the summer in Israel. There she had met a boy from Washington Heights—the well-known Orthodox neighborhood in Upper Manhattan—and by the time they had both returned to New York from a summer of study in Jerusalem, it had been decided that they would get married. The engagement party was to be held on Monday evening in the catering hall of the synagogue, and of course, Devora and her family were among those invited.

But that Monday afternoon, only hours before the party was to begin, trouble struck. Shira came to Devora's house and walked into her friend's room. Devora was at her desk doing her homework.

"Devora," Shira told her, "you have to help my family." She was almost crying.

"What's wrong?" Devora asked. "What happened?"

"My father is in the hospital," said Shira. "Some kids out in the street threw a firecracker at him. He fainted, and now he's in the hospital."

Devora tried to calm her friend. "What can I do? Do you want me to go to the hospital with you and your mother?"

Shira shook her head. "No, it's not that, Devora. You see, my father picked out four diamonds—they're beautiful—one for each of us four sisters, for the time we get engaged. This morning, after morning services at *shul,* he went with my brother, Yoel, to the bank to take the four diamonds from his safe deposit box so that Chana and her fiancé could choose the one they wanted to have set in a ring for Chana. My father had the diamonds somewhere on him, but nobody knows where. When the ambulance picked him up, Yoel looked whether the diamonds had fallen into the street, but they weren't there. At the hospital, he searched through my father's clothes, but no diamonds." She swallowed hard and blew her nose. "The doctor says Daddy will be all right, and, although he is now under sedation, he'll probably be home tomorrow. But meanwhile we have to find out what happened to the diamonds. Maybe they did fall out in the street. Anybody could pick them up. But maybe they're still somewhere in my father's clothes. Yoel saw Sergeant O'Malley in the hospital, and told him about the diamonds. The sergeant went through the clothes, but couldn't find anything!"

Devora looked bewildered.

"How can I help?" she asked.

"I told my brother to bring the clothes to you," Shira replied. "I told him you could find anything!"

Devora blushed. This was not the kind of praise she liked. "If your brother and Sergeant O'Malley weren't able to find the diamonds, I don't know whether I'll do any better than they," she said.

Just then, the doorbell rang. Shira jumped from her chair. "It must be them!" she cried excitedly.

Downstairs, *Rebbe* Doresh had just opened the door to let in Yoel Hellman and Sergeant O'Malley. As Devora entered the living room, Yoel and the sergeant nodded to her. Mr. Hellman's clothes and belongings were lying spread out on a table.

"First," *Rebbe* Doresh began, "maybe we'd better have Yoel tell Devora everything that happened before his father's accident."

"What's there to say?" Yoel shrugged his shoulders. A tall, slim boy of 15, he was obviously upset. His sister had insisted that he come to Devora. He had thought the idea was silly but finally decided that it was worth a try. But now, at Devora's house, he felt silly all over again. "What's there to say?" he repeated. "We went to *shul,* and from there to the bank to pick up the diamonds."

"Did your father say anything to you after you left the bank?" Devora asked.

"Well . . . when he came out of the cubicle after taking the diamonds from the safe deposit box, he laughed and told me he had found the best possible hiding place for the diamonds. But he never had a chance to tell me where."

Slowly and carefully, Devora began to go through Mr. Hellman's clothes. Sergeant O'Malley gave her a patronizing smile as he watched her work. "I don't know why you have to go through all that stuff again," he said to Devora. "We even checked his bag." He pointed at Mr. Hellman's blue velvet *tallith** bag. Devora picked up the bag and opened the zipper. Slowly, she removed the contents of the bag, one by one. First, the long, white *tallith*. She carefully unfolded the *tallith,* then folded it again and placed it on the table. Next, she took out the two *tefillin*.** Then came the prayerbook, and finally the *Humash,* the Bible which Mr. Hellman carried with him to *shul* each morning. Devora opened the *Humash* and leafed through its pages. The black silk marker remained in place at the end of the portion that had been read on the Sabbath before, and again on that Monday morning. For a

---

*Prayer shawl
**Phylacteries — small black leather boxes containing sacred scrolls, worn on the arm and head during morning prayers.

moment, Rabbi Epstein's sermon of two days before came back to her. She kissed the *Humash* and closed it again. Next, she opened the prayerbook, leafing through it carefully, before closing it again and placing it on the table next to Mr. Hellman's *tallith* bag.

Yoel Hellman was talking again. "When my father came out of the cubicle at the bank, there was one other thing he told me. 'My son,' he said, 'be proud that you're a religious Jew and are observing all the commandments of the Torah.' But Daddy knows I'm proud to be Jewish. So why should he have told me that at the bank of all places?"

"Proud to be Jewish." Devora gave Yoel a quick look. "Did you check your father's *yarmulke?*" she asked him. "I mean, did you feel inside the lining of the *yarmulke?*"

Sergeant O'Malley grinned. "I had the same idea. I looked over that *yarmulke* at the hospital. But I couldn't feel any diamonds there."

Shira was starting to cry again. Devora went over to put her arms around her friend. In the meantime, Yoel slowly began to put everything back into the *tallith* bag.

"Wait!" Devora cried suddenly. She ran over to the *tallith* bag and pulled out the *Humash* again. She opened the book to the place where the marker was resting. "And the Lord spoke to Moses," she began to read. "Speak to the Children of Israel and command them to make for themselves . . . fringes in the corners of their garments. . . . And it shall be a fringe for you, so that you may look upon it, and remember all the commandments of the Lord, and observe them . . . " Devora walked back to the table and picked up Mr. Hellman's *tzitzith*. The four-cornered fringed garment hung loosely in her left hand, while the fingers of her right hand made their way to the fringes. The fringes of each corner were inserted into a square piece of material sewn onto the corner of the garment, very much like a patch of reinforcement. Devora felt each corner patch. Then, from behind each patch, she withdrew a small piece of cotton. Inside each of the four balls of cotton there was a beautiful, glittering round diamond.

Sergeant O'Malley gaped and gave a low whistle. Yoel stared at the *tzitzith,* his mouth wide open. Shira Hellman laughed nervously. *Rebbe* Doresh fairly beamed. "How did you know, Devora?" he asked.

"Well, *Abba,**" she said to her father. "This past Shabbos we were reading the portion about the commandment of wearing *tzitzith*. The *tzitzith* has four corners—just enough room for four diamonds."

Sergeant O'Malley's eyes narrowed. "Well, I suppose it takes one of you Jewish yeshiva girls to figure that one out," he conceded with just a touch of admiration in his gruff voice.

*Father

Mystery of the Secret Code

ebbe Doresh knocked on his daughter's bedroom door. "Devora!" he called to her. "Could you come out for a few minutes? There are some people in the living room waiting to see you."

Devora opened the door and followed her father into the living room. Sergeant O'Malley was there, waiting. With him were two younger men. One of them, the taller of the two, wore a hat; the other was bareheaded. The stranger without the hat looked angrily at Devora, then at his companion. "Look!" he shouted, "This is just a child! It's a real waste of time!"

"Take it easy, Benjamin," the man with the hat soothed him. "She may be a child, but she's not exactly a dummy. You'll see." Devora recognized this man; he had a house a block from the synagogue.

The two men and Sergeant O'Malley sat down on the living room sofa. Then the man with the hat began to speak. "This man here," he said, gesturing with his hand to the other visitor, "is Mr. Benjamin Small. He has a problem which he already took to the police department. Unfortunately it looks like the police can't handle it alone."

Mr. Benjamin Small got up nervously and sat down

on a chair across from the sofa. "My father and my uncle are business partners," he explained. "Every year one of them goes to Belgium on business while the other stays home. This year, for some reason, both of them went together. I haven't heard from either of them since they left. My father always writes or calls me when he's away. My uncle has no family of his own; whenever he travels alone, he writes to my father, or to me. But this time both of them left together and they didn't leave me a list of the places where they were going. That is, they may have left a list in the—"

"This thing beats me," Sergeant O'Malley cut in. "I thought I'd heard of everything under the sun, but it turns out I sure didn't. Mr. Small here tells me that his father and his uncle don't trust banks to keep their valuables safe. So they got together a couple of business friends, and they went ahead and built their own vault. In this vault, each man has his own safe deposit box. There's a private guard whom they all pay. Mr. Small thinks that this is the place where his father and uncle may have left a list of cities they intended to visit in Belgium. There is something even more strange: most combination locks on safes have only three numbers, but the safe deposit box of the Small brothers has four. And this is where the real trouble comes in; those Small brothers seem to like talking in riddles . . . "

"Before my father and my uncle left on their trip," Mr. Benjamin Small resumed his story, "my father gave me an envelope. He said that the combination of the safe was on a slip of paper inside. My father can be quite dramatic—and, as the Sergeant just said, he likes communicating in riddles. So I just stuffed the envelope into my pants and forgot about it. But by now I'm worried. I haven't heard a word from either my father or my uncle. They're both well up in years-close to seventy, and Belgium isn't exactly a little village. Besides, they might have made a side trip to Holland or Germany. So I can't really expect the police to do very much unless I can supply them with at least some information about the travel plans my father and my uncle had. And now it turns out that the slip inside the envelope my father gave me doesn't have the combination numbers on it but just another riddle. You see, my father was one of those super-smart yeshiva students back in the old country, so he enjoys riddles and thinks I should enjoy them, too. But apparently the one thing he never figured on is that he and my uncle would end up being a mystery themselves . . ."

Devora had been listening quietly all the time, looking intently at Mr. Small, then at Sergeant O'Malley.

"How come the police can't help?" she finally asked.

"Because the riddle is in Hebrew, that's why," the Sergeant replied.

"Could I see the slip, please?"

"Okay, Devora Know-It-All. Here it is," said Sergeant O'Malley.

Devora looked at the writing on the paper and read it aloud to the others:

> *"Aleph Beis Gimmel Daled*
> Small ben Yamin Small
> Your House."

She turned the paper over. "Is that all the information your father left you, Mr. Small?"

"Yes, Devora. That's what he gave me. And I
remember he said I'd be able to figure out the numbers
of the combination easily enough. Well, I can't, not for
the life of me. There are three lines on this slip, but I
know that the combination has four numbers. Now of
course, *Aleph, Beis, Gimmel,* and *Daled* aren't only the
first four letters of the Hebrew alphabet, but also repre-
sent the numbers 1,2,3 and 4. Well, I tried that one,
already. But the combination is not 1,2,3,4."

Devora looked at the slip of paper again. "Your
name is Mr. Small," she said. "And our neighbor here
called you Benjamin. Is that your first name?"

"Yes, it is," said Mr. Small.

"Now then, why did your father spell your first
name in such a strange way? 'ben Yamin'? No capital B,
but a capital Y, and he made two words out of your first
name. And oh, yes, what could he have meant by writing 'your house'? Maybe he means that he left the list of
places not in the safe but at the house where you live.
Could he have done that?"

"I've turned my house upside down. Didn't find
anything. I have also searched through my father's
house and my uncle's place, too. There is no locked
drawer anywhere, or any box with a combination
lock."

"What's your house number?" Devora asked.

Mr. Small leaned back and looked at her. "It's a
1435. 1435 Angles Avenue!" he exclaimed. "My father
wrote, 'Your house.' Do you think he meant the com-

bination is the same as my house number? But then, why *Aleph, Beis, Gimmel, Daled,* and the funny spelling of my name?"

Devora shook her head. "I don't think your father meant that the combination is the same as the number of your house. It might be worth trying, though. But before you do that, could you tell me a little about your father?"

"What for?"

"Because it might help answer our questions about *Aleph, Beis, Gimmel, Daled,* and about the way he wrote out your name."

"Well, you already know that he was an old-world yeshiva student. He always hoped we boys would follow in the same path—go to yeshiva, study Torah. Go into business or some profession, okay, but spend your spare time studying the Talmud. My brother and I have done plenty of studying, but it wasn't the Talmud. I am a professor of English, and my brother is a scientist down in Texas. Our father could never understand how I got involved with English literature instead of Hebrew. But then, you see, I'm not religious. My father's religious values just don't work in this day and age—at least that's what I think."

Rebbe Doresh walked over to the living room window. He looked out into the street, then turned around and said:

"To my way of thinking, religion today is more important than ever . . ."

But Mr. Small was not in a mood for listening to *Rebbe* Doresh. "Look, Rabbi," he said, "I may not agree with my father about religion, but I love him very much. I want him found. And I have to learn the four numbers of his safe deposit box combination so I can open it and find out his travel route in Belgium. Can your daughter help me in this thing or not? That's all I'm interested in knowing. Sergeant O'Malley here, and your neighbor, both, suggested that I come to you for help. I'm ready to try anything. Now I'll make one more trip to the vault and try the numbers of my address–1,4,3,5."

He got up from his chair and moved toward the door, but Devora stopped him. "Just a minute, please. May I copy the message on the slip your father left you? I want to think about it some more."

"Sure." Mr. Small handed her the slip to copy.

Later that day, at supper time, Mr. Small telephoned. The numbers 1,4,3,5 had not worked. "Better think of something else, young lady," he told Devora. "I asked Sergeant O'Malley to have the lock forced open, but he said he can't do that until three months from now. But we have to know earlier than that. If we can't find out about my father's travel route, it'll take the police that much longer to find my father and my uncle. And right now, speed means everything. These two men are old. Who knows—"

After Devora had hung up the receiver, Mrs. Doresh had something to say. "If it is the will of G-d that Mr. Small's father and uncle turn up safe and sound, then they'll be all right. But you know, Devora, you can't spend all your time on Mr. Small's problem.

As far as I could see, you haven't started your homework as yet. So, you'd better go to your room and do your homework. Afterwards, you can go back to thinking about Mr. Small's troubles."

Devora went to her room and sat down at her desk, but she was unable to concentrate on her studies for long. Again and again, her mind went back to the numbers and the letters in the note from Mr. Small's father. Numbers and letters. . . . In Hebrew, all the letters of the alphabet also stand for numbers. Each of the girls in her class had a code name, consisting of the numbers represented by the Hebrew letters in their names. The Hebrew letters in Devora's name was *Daled, Beis, Vav, Resh* and *He,* and so her code name was 4,2,6,200,5.

Once again, she looked at the message she had copied, from the slip in Mr. Small's envelope. She studied it quietly, tapping her pencil eraser against her forehead. Old Mr. Small wanted his son to study the Hebrew language. Perhaps he even wanted him to think in Hebrew, and figured that the best way to make him do so was to leave him with a mysterious message which only a student of Hebrew would be able to figure out. "*Aleph, Beis, Gimmel, Daled,*" she read. Then she went on to the second line of the message, "Small ben Yamin Small." Devora circled the word 'Yamin.' Why hadn't she thought of it before? Yamin was the Hebrew word for "right" or "to the right." So far, so good. But why had the old gentleman repeated his last name *twice?* Suddenly it came to her. Perhaps the word

"Small" in this message was not meant to be Benjamin's last name, but an English way of spelling *S'mol,* the Hebrew for "left" or "to the left." Could all this be a direction for turning the combination lock—left, then right, then left again? But if so, then what about the third line, "Your house"? What was the Hebrew for "your house"? It was *beis-cha,* a word with four letters—*Beis* equalling 2, *Yud* equalling 10, *Saph* equalling 400 and the last letter, *Chaph,* equalling 20. Following a sudden idea, she crossed out all the zeroes after each number, so that the numbers left were 2, 1, 4 and 2. Left, then right, then left again, and 2, 1, 4 and 2. It made very good sense. She put it all down on a sheet of yellow paper.

She got up, went into her father's study, and showed him her yellow sheet. *Rebbe* Doresh immediately put aside the book of rabbinic thoughts he had been reading, and dialed the telephone number of Mr. Benjamin Small.

Within twenty-four hours the mystery had been solved. Devora had found the correct combination. Mr. Small had opened up the safe and found his father's travel route there. And a few hours later, Mr. Small received word that his father and uncle were all right. It seemed that his father had given the uncle a letter to mail to America, but the uncle, a rather absent-minded old man, had thrown the letter into a trash can instead of a mail box. Both father and uncle were safe and sound in Knokke, a Belgian seaside resort where many Jewish people traveled for weekends and longer vacations.

Several days later, Mr. Small came to visit at the Doresh home, bringing with him a box of candy for the entire family. "Don't worry," he said to Mrs. Doresh, "I made sure this candy is kosher. And, by the way, I think I've decided to turn over a new leaf. I'll study Hebrew myself so if my father or my uncle start talking in riddles again, I'll be able to do the same thing with them. And maybe I'll start studying about Judaism again while I'm at it. Religion seems to be working all right for my father, my uncle, and for the four of you. Perhaps in the end it'll work for me as well."

The Dangerous Doctor

Mrs. Sara Freida Hoffman was standing in the toy department of Macy's, examining a wind-up toy for her youngest son, Yitzhak, who had just turned three. Holding the furry wind-up dog, she pictured the look of pure joy that appeared on Yitzhak's face whenever he received a gift. She had already bought three gifts, one for each of her small sons. Months ago she had decided to have toys ready for her children to bring back with her from the hospital, along with their live new baby brother or sister. For David, her seven-year-old, she had chosen a game. Moshe, the five-year-old, was more studious, so she had bought him a set of books.

She took a deep breath and started out for the next aisle where her niece, Devora Doresh, had been waiting. Mrs. Hoffman smiled to herself. Her husband, Aaron Hoffman, had not wanted her to go shopping by herself when the new baby was expected so soon. So Devora had offered to join her aunt because there had been no school that morning. Little Yitzhak was sleeping at Mrs. Doresh's house, the two older boys were at yeshiva, and so Devora and Mrs. Hoffman had the whole morning ahead of them.

Suddenly, Mrs. Hoffman leaned heavily against the counter.

"Are you all right, Aunt Sara Freida?" Devora asked.

"I . . . think so . . ." Mrs. Hoffman replied, "but I also think I'm ready to go to the hospital."

Devora asked one of the salesgirls for a chair and had her aunt sit down. Then she rushed into the elevator and out in the street for a taxicab. From then on, things went so fast that Devora later could hardly remember how she and her aunt had made it to the hospital. After Mrs. Hoffman had been placed upon a stretcher and had disappeared behind the swinging doors marked "Emergency" Devora went to the nearest telephone to call her mother.

"Good girl," Mrs. Doresh said after Devora had told her what had happened. "Now stay right where you are until Uncle Aaron gets there. When he does, you'll come home and help take care of little Yitzhak."

Devora hung up the receiver and turned to the nurse nearby. But the nurse was busy filling in some forms and did not even look up when Devora asked her the way to the Maternity Department.

And that was how Devora suddenly found herself in the corridor leading to Maternity. "Come on, get into your uniform!" someone shouted at her, pointing to a read and white smock hanging on a hook on the wall. It was the candy striped uniform for young girl volunteer helpers. Apparently someone had mistaken her for somebody else, because she, Devora, had never worked

at the hospital before. But she took the smock off the hook, tried it on and looked into the mirror. She liked herself in the uniform. Maybe she would become a volunteer worker and help bring cheer to the patients. But she reminded herself that there was plenty for her to do at school, and then, of course, there was the "Lost-and-Found" bureau . . .

"Devora!" It was Uncle Aaron. "Where's your Aunt Sara? Is everything all right?"

Just then a pair of big doors opened wide and out came the doctor. It was Dr. Ari Berman, who had been there also when each of Aunt Sara's three sons had been born. He took off his surgical mask and cap, and wiped his forehead with a tissue. He was all smiles. "Mazel Tov," he said to Uncle Aaron. "You finally got it! This time it's a girl, and a gorgeous little girl at that."

Aaron Hoffman was delighted. He was proud of his three sons, but he and Aunt Sara had always wanted a daughter, too. Now their happiness would be complete.

"Congratulations," said Dr. Hubert Carey. He, too, pulled off his mask, and then his cap. "I heard you finally got the little girl you wanted."

Suddenly Devora heard her name called from the far end of the corridor. "Devorah Doresh! What in the Sam Hill are you doing here?" Sergeant O'Malley was coming toward her. But before Devora was able to answer him, the big doors swung open again and out came Dr. Steven Marshall. "So you had a little girl? Well, my congratulations to you and the wife!" he shouted jovially. Like the two other doctors, he, too, had taken off his cap. But his surgical mask remained in place. He tapped his feet as he whistled a tune. "The first dance in honor of the little princess," he sang out.

To Devora's surprise, Sergeant O'Malley was not smiling. In fact, he looked pale and grim. Devora had not seen such a look on his face before. "I'm glad you serious-minded doctors are in such a good mood. Now perhaps you gentlemen will tell me which one of you I'm after?"

"Is there anything wrong, officer?" Dr. Marshall asked.

"There certainly is," the police officer replied. "One of your orderlies was found in the room next to yours—dead. Murdered, to be exact."

"You must be joking," Dr. Marshall stammered.

"I wish it was a joke," said Sergeant O'Malley, "I happened to have known him personally—John Giorgio. He was a good man . . . and I'm going to get the guy who did it."

"Do you have a suspect?" Devora asked.

"Yes," said the sergeant. "We suspect one of the doctors in this hospital."

There was a shocked silence. All three doctors looked upset. Dr. Berman was the first to recover his composure.

"That's a pretty serious charge to make," he said. "What basis do you have for such an accusation?"

"Look, Doctor Berman," Sergeant O'Malley replied, "John Giorgio wasn't exactly a hospital orderly by profession. He was one of the best undercover

policemen we had in our squad. We found out from
him quite a while ago that one of the doctors in this
department has been stealing drugs from the hospital
supply rooms and selling them. One of the doctors right
in this department is a drug king. As a matter of fact,
Giorgio called me only an hour ago and told me he had
finally found the one. But by the time I could get here,
whoever it was managed to get rid of Giorgio."

Sergeant O'Malley turned to Devora. "How long
have you been here?"

Devora shrugged her shoulders. "Not long enough
to have seen anything."

"Aren't you working here?" the sergeant asked,
pointing to the candy-striped smock she was wearing.

Devora shook her head and looked embarrassed as
she unbuttoned the smock. It slipped off like a duster
and she hung it back on the hook from which she had
taken it. She looked at her Uncle Aaron. "I think I'd
better go home," she said. "to take care of little Yitzhak
so my mother can come here."

Uncle Aaron nodded his head. It seemed strange to
be talking about death and a new life at the same time.
He shuddered.

At home, Devora put away the three gifts Aunt Sara
Freida had bought for her sons at Macy's. Then she
turned to play with little Yitzhak, who had just
awakened from his nap. Mrs. Doresh had already left
for the hospital.

Before long, the phone rang. It was Mrs. Doresh.
Everything was fine. She would be coming home very

soon. "It's only 3 o'clock," she told Devora, "so you can still go back to school and stay for the special class in *Shulhan Arukh* later on." The *Shulhan Arukh* is the code which lists all the hundreds of laws and regulations every observant Jew must try to follow. Devora had been looking forward eagerly to the special class *Morah* Hartman was going to give after school hours that day.

"Sergeant O'Malley was nice enough to offer me a ride home," Mrs. Doresh continued, "and now he says that if you're ready, he'll drive you to school."

Devora went to her room, prepared her school books and then she remembered Yitzhak. She found him under the kitchen table, crying.

"My car! I lost it!"

"Where did you put it?" Devora asked.

"Here!" The little boy said, pointing to the floor.

Together, Devora and Yitzhak looked in the living room and the dining room. But there was no trace of Yitzhak's little red car.

"If only you would keep things in order," she said, more to herself than to Yitzhak, "then you'd know where you put it. There's a place for everything, but we have to know it."

She went into the kitchen, peeled a long thin carrot and offered it to Yitzhak. The little boy stopped crying and began to munch on the carrot.

Devora heard a car horn honking outside, and then the doorbell ringing. Her mother came in and wished her Mazel Tov on her new little cousin. Sergeant O'Malley was outside, waiting in the car for Devora.

Devora climbed into the car and closed the door.

The sergeant started the car. "Are you sure you didn't see anything unusual at the hospital?" he asked her, without taking his eyes from the road. "Sometimes you appear to see things the rest of us ordinary people never notice."

"I'm sorry, Sergeant," Devorah answered, "but if I will remember something I'll be sure to tell you. Crime isn't my field—not yet at least." She tried to smile, but couldn't, because she was sorry Sergeant O'Malley had lost his friend, John Giorgio.

"Well," Sergeant O'Malley said after some minutes of quiet. "We do know that there was a struggle, and that during the struggle, Giorgio tore the clothes of the doctor who did it. We haven't found all the torn garments yet, but we already have some scraps of material from a surgical uniform." Then he stopped. A few moments went by before he spoke again. "Now I want you to keep under your hat what I'm about to tell you. Maybe I shouldn't be talking to you about it, but here it is. When you and I were at the hospital this morning, we saw three doctors—Dr. Berman, Dr. Carey and Dr. Marshall. One of these three doctors did it. We only have to find out which one."

Devora was shocked. Surely not Dr. Berman! He had been a good friend of her Uncle Aaron's; after all, he'd been there when David, Moshe and Yitzhak had been born. And now he'd been the first to see Aunt Sara Freida's little girl . . .

"Here we are!" Sergeant O'Malley interrupted Devora's thoughts. "Out you go, young lady."

Devora thanked the sergeant, climbed out of the car and entered the building of the Yocheved High School. She went to her classroom, opened the door quietly, and stepped in. *Morah* Hartman had already begun her talk on the *Shulhan Arukh. Morah* Hartman had seen Devora through the classroom window getting out of Sergeant O'Malley's car. Out on a case again, that *Gemora Kop,* she sighed to herself.

"Please open your books, girls," she was saying. "We will start by reviewing the table of contents of the *Shulhan Arukh.* All the laws a good Jew is supposed to obey are arranged in this book—from the time you get up in the morning until you go to bed at night. There's a separate section for the holidays, and another section for how to be an honest businessman. Every law has been set down in the proper section. Each law has its own place. Do you know the translation for the title of this book—*Shulhan Arukh?* Literally, it means, 'The Prepared Table.' Just as a dinner table is set in a certain order—plates here, knives and forks there, spoons in another place, serving dishes in the center—so , too, our lives as Jews and as human beings under the law of G-d must be arranged in strict order."

Morah Hartman turned the page of her book. "You know, girls, everything about Jewish law has order in it. One thing follows the other, always in the same succession, never the other way around. Take the laws of Passover, for instance. The first two nights of Pesach we have the *seder.* Now girls, what's the English word for *seder?"*

"Order!" the girls shouted.

"Yes," said *Morah* Hartman. "The Hagaddah which we use at the *seder* table shows us the order in which we are to observe the evening. First the Four Questions, then the answers, then the first bite of matzo, then the meal, then the prayers of thanksgiving and then, in the end, the songs like *Had Gadya.*"

Devora was shifting in her seat. Something was bothering her but she did not yet know what.

"Anything wrong, Devora?" *Morah* Hartman asked. "No, Ma'am," Devora answered, but somehow she was no longer able to concentrate on what her teacher was telling the class.

When she returned home, she found all her three cousins, David, Moshe and Yitzhak Hoffman at the house.

"Want my red car!" Yitzhak whined.

There it was! Only a few hours ago Devora had told Yitzhak to keep his things in order, and now *Morah* Hartman had spent a whole lesson explaining how everything in Jewish law was listed in strict order, and that, in fact, there must be order in everything we do in life.

Devora walked into the kitchen, where her mother was preparing dinner. "May I go back to the hospital, Mother?" she asked. "I think I remember something."

Mrs. Doresh nodded. "All right, Devora but whatever it is you remember, please don't forget about your homework for tomorrow!"

Sergeant O'Malley was back at the hospital too. "Are you going in to visit your aunt?" he asked Devora.

"Yes, Sergeant, I am, but there's something else, too," she said.

"Did you come up with something since our ride this afternoon?" the officer demanded.

"Yes, I did. This afternoon at school my teacher talked about the order in which the laws of our religion are arranged, and she kept saying that there should be a set order for all the things we do, from the time we get up until the time we are ready to go to sleep. So there is order also in the things the doctors do in hospitals."

"Meaning what?" Sergeant O'Malley was looking intently at Devora.

"Not too long ago I read a book about a famous surgeon, and I recall the order in which the nurse helped him into his surgical clothes. First came the gown, then the cap, and only then she tied the surgical mask around his head. I suppose the mask goes on last so the doctor can take it off first when he goes into the waiting room after the operation to talk to the family of the patient. It's easier to take off the mask when it is tied over the cap."

Sergeant O'Malley nodded. Yes, all this made sense, but what did it have to do with the doctors who were suspects in the murder of John Giorgio?

"You said that John put up a fight and tore the clothes of the doctor who attacked him," Devora continued. "Now listen to this, Sergeant O'Malley: When Dr. Berman and Dr. Carey came out of the operating room, they took off their masks first, and their caps only afterwards. But Dr. Marshall still had his mask on, although he had taken off his cap. Didn't you notice that, Sergeant?"

"And so—"

"I think that when John Giorgio tried to fight the doctor who killed him, he ripped the mask off the doctor's face. After John was dead, the doctor who did it thought he'd better go and straighten himself up. He went to the men's room and brushed his hair, so nobody would see he'd been in a fight. Then he looked for another surgical mask to put on with his cap. But this time he didn't have a nurse to help him. So, instead of putting on his cap first and the mask last, he put his mask on first and his cap only after that. When he came out and saw you, he tried to act cheerful and innocent. He started congratulating my uncle and going into a dance 'in honor of the little princess,' he said. But I saw there was something not quite right about the way he was dressed. He had his cap off, but his mask was still tied around his face. So now you see which one of the three doctors must have killed John Giorgio."

"Steven Marshall!" Sergeant O'Malley exclaimed. He gripped the holster in which he carried his gun, then gritted his teeth. "Just let me at him! It won't bring John Giorgio back to his wife and baby but at least that doctor won't ever be able to kill anyone else, not for a long, long time!"

Devora nodded silently. "I guess I'll have to go now, Sergeant O'Malley," she said. "It's getting late and I still want to see my aunt and her new little girl."

A Purim Mystery

evora! Good! I'm glad you're home already. Mother and I have been waiting for you." *Rebbe* Doresh opened the door to greet his daughter, who had just come home from school. "I don't want to rush you, but I was just leaving to pay a condolence call. It's Mr. Aaron Cohen, from down the avenue. His wife, Goldie, died a few days ago, and he's sitting *shiva*.* I'd like to go to his house in time for the afternoon service, and Mother wants to come with me. Would you like to join us?"

Devora wanted very much to go. She had known Mrs. Cohen as one of the ladies who was very involved in the Yocheved School. Mrs. Cohen had had no children of her own, so she had looked upon the girls at Yocheved as her daughters. Mr. Cohen was just the opposite. He hardly ever stopped to speak to anyone at the synagogue or in the neighborhood. Mrs. Cohen had always smiled, but Mr. Cohen never did, at least not as far as anyone knew. Devora had always wondered how the two had ever gotten along.

Four days earlier, Mrs. Cohen had been rushed to the hospital with a heart attack. Several hours later, she was dead.

*Seven days of mourning

Mrs. Doresh came into the living room and put on her coat. "Poor Mr. Cohen," she sighed. "This was his second wife, and now he's all alone in the world."

Mr. Cohen had been one of the fortunate Jews who had been able to leave Russia many years ago. But beyond that, he had had very little joy in his life. During the years after World War II, Mr. Cohen and his brother Feivel had not done badly in Russia. They had had a good education and well-paying jobs. Feivel had worked as a jewelry designer. Mr. Cohen had been an architect and, because of his work, he even had been permitted to travel outside the country from time to time. He had a wife and four daughters. His only sorrow then had been that the girls were not receiving a Jewish education, but he had hoped that someday the dictator, Josef Stalin, would permit Jews to study their Judaism openly once more as they had done for hundreds of years before the Revolution. Instead, Stalin had suddenly turned his anger on the Jews. One night, the Secret Police knocked on the door of Mr. Cohen's apartment. He was arrested, tried and sentenced to hard labor in Siberia. Miraculously, he survived the back-breaking toil and the bitter cold. When Stalin died, Mr. Cohen was told that he could go home. When he returned to his home in Kiev, he learned that his family was gone. Neighbors informed him that his wife had been taken away by the Secret Police. Later, he learned that she had been shot. No one knew what had become of his four daughters. They seemed to have vanished into thin air.

For years, Mr. Cohen searched for his daughters, but in vain. He was allowed to take up his work as an architect again, but the joy had gone out of his life. Then, he was sent to a conference in Hungary. While he was there, the Hungarians revolted and thousands of Jews fled across the border into the free world. Among them was Mr. Cohen. From America, he hoped, he might be able to learn what had become of his daughters, and of his brother, Feivel.

Unfortunately, Mr. Cohen did not prosper in New York. There were plenty of architects in the city, and he was no longer young. He got a job in an office and for years lived in a furnished room, to which he returned every evening after work. It was a very lonely life. When he met Goldie Minzer, a widow from Boro Park, he was taken by her warmth and vivaciousness. They were married and settled down in Goldie's house. But to Mr. Cohen's sorrow, they had no children. Goldie had never had children, but he, Mr. Cohen, had once had four daughters, and he still could not believe that they all were dead. And now Goldie, who had never even had a cold as long as he had known her, was gone . . .

When Devora Doresh and her parents arrived at Mr. Cohen's house, only a few other visitors were there. The mirrors and pictures on the wall were covered with sheets and towels as a sign of mourning. Mr. Cohen sat on a low stool in front of the dining room cupboard, his head in his hands. He got up when *Rebbe* Doresh entered the room, but *Rebbe* Doresh motioned to him to remain seated, and sat down on a chair close to Mr. Cohen. Mrs. Doresh and Devora pulled up two more chairs for themselves.

"So, *Rebbe* Doresh," Mr. Cohen sighed. "What will become of me now? Everything I touch seems to die. It almost seems as if G-d was not pleased with me."

Rebbe Doresh said nothing, but waited for Mr. Cohen to go on talking.

"You know, I once told you about my brother Feivel," Mr. Cohen continued. "The jewelry designer? Do you remember, he designed rings for my daughters . . ." He turned to Devora with a sad smile. "I had four daughters in Russia, each one named after a matriarch in the Bible—Sara, Rebecca, Rachel and Leah. So Feivel designed a ring for each of them with a Biblical theme. One ring for each girl—beautiful rings. My line used to be architecture, not jewelry. . . . But only last week, I promised Goldie that I would buy her a beautiful ring, a gold ring, with any design she wanted. We even ordered the ring . . . but Goldie won't ever wear it now. . . ."

By that time several neighbors had arrived, and the men were ready to begin afternoon prayers. Devora and her mother went into the kitchen. Mrs. Doresh opened the bag of groceries she had bought for Mr. Cohen.

After the brief service in the dining room had ended, Mrs. Doresh prepared a light supper for Mr. Cohen. After he had eaten, the Doresh family went home.

Several days later, *Rebbe* Doresh received a letter from Israel. It came from Yosef Goren, who many years ago had studied together with *Rebbe* Doresh at a yeshiva on the Lower East Side. Later, he had gone to a university and studied archeology. Throughout the years, Dr. Goren and *Rebbe* Doresh had remained good friends. Then, soon after the war of 1967, Mr. Goren and his family had left America to settle in Israel. In Jerusalem, he found important work as an archeologist. It made Dr. Goren happy that some of his archeological finds helped prove to the world that the stories in the Torah were based on fact. Many of his letters to *Rebbe* Doresh were detailed accounts of discoveries he had made.

This time, however, his letter was a request for a favor. One of his students, a young woman, was going to be sent from Israel to New York to do research at a museum. The girl knew no one in the United States. She was not religious, but Mr. Goren wanted the Doresh family to take her into their home for the few weeks she was going to spend in New York. "Perhaps meeting you and staying with you will give Sara a better understanding of our tradition," he wrote. At the same time, he felt, the Doresh family would find it interesting to talk with the visitor from Israel.

On the day Sara was scheduled to arrive, *Rebbe* Doresh and Devora drove to the airport to meet her. Devora had agreed to share her room with the visitor; her bed was a hi-riser which could easily be opened to accommodate a guest.

Devora and her father were able to pick the visitor almost immediately from the crowd of arriving passengers. Tall and thin, with dark hair and a dark complexion, Sara Aviv looked like a typical Israeli. She gave Devora a broad smile, showing sparkling white teeth.

"Shalom!" she said, "Thank you for coming to the airport to meet me. I also appreciate your invitation to be your guest. I wanted to stay with Jewish people. You see, I've never been here before."

"You speak a beautiful English," said Devora with a warm smile. She had taken an instant liking to Sara. Dr. Goren had written that Sara Aviv was about 30 years old and very intelligent, so Devora had expected someone very formal and serious. Now she was delighted to find Sara a warm and vibrant person. Devora was sure that she and Sara would become friends.

All through the ride to the Doresh home, Sara Aviv was bubbling over with enthusiasm. "This is my first trip away from Israel," she explained. "So when I was asked whether I wanted to do some work in this country, I was all excited. My friends were all thrilled for me. You see, I live at the Hebrew University. They gave me a farewell party. Oh, yes, and they told me to beware of American men."

Rebbe Doresh looked straight in front of him at the road, but laughed and gave her a wink through the mirror. "My friend Dr. Goren told me the same thing. He said I mustn't introduce you to any American men

unless it's someone who'd be willing to live in Israel.
Dr. Goren likes you too much to lose you from his
working team."

Sara laughed. "Actually, *Rebbe* Doresh, I'm here to
work and not to find a husband. But who knows . . ."

By the time the day was over, Devora had come to
the conclusion that Sara was a wonderful guest. She
even offered to help Mrs. Doresh dry the dishes, a job
Devora did every night but hated.

Sara did not seem the least tired after the long flight
from Israel. She was up early the next morning, ready
to report to the museum. "I'm going to Manhattan
myself later this morning," Mrs. Doresh said. "Maybe
we could take the subway together, so you won't get
lost."

Sara smiled. "I'd love to come with you, Mrs.
Doresh, but I promised to be at the museum early.
Don't worry. I'll find my way."

Every evening Sara came straight home from the
museum full of stories about the exciting things she had
seen and learned. But one evening, she was late. When
she finally arrived, it was seven o'clock, and there was a
policeman with her. As soon as she entered the house,
she threw herself down on the sofa. Her face was
white.

"What happened?" Mrs. Doresh asked, badly
frightened.

"Don't be upset," the policeman said. "The young
lady's going to be fine. But she had an unpleasant
experience at the Museum today. Somebody attacked

her at the museum."

Mrs. Doresh and Devora looked at Sara, then at each other.

"You see, she was working at the museum," the policeman went on, "when, out of the clear blue sky, some crazy old man grabbed her arm and yelled at her. 'Murderer!' that's what he called her. Then he escaped before anybody was able to stop him."

Rebbe Doresh had entered the room. "Now why should anyone call Miss Aviv a murderer, I wonder? The man must have been sick . . ."

"I don't know," said Sara. She could barely speak above a whisper, and her hands were shaking.

"Exactly what were you doing when the man attacked you?" Devora asked gently.

"We were taking pictures of some objects in the Persian Room of the museum. I was holding a spear and a shield for the photographer . . ."

The policeman nodded. "I guess when that man saw you holding that spear, Miss, you reminded him of something frightening from his past."

"Perhaps you should stay home tomorrow, Sara," Mrs. Doresh volunteered. "After that shock, you need a day's rest."

"Oh, no, Mrs. Doresh, I mustn't let myself go like that," said Sara, trying to sound cheerful. "I'm feeling much better already. I think he was probably a drunk— a drunk old man. He looked bad. Needed a shave, too. . . ."

"But we want you to be all right by tomorrow

evening," *Rebbe* Doresh cut in. "You know, it'll be Purim, and everyone is supposed to be in good spirits then."

The next morning, Mrs. Doresh was baking *haman-tashen** for the following day's Purim party when she was interrupted by the telephone. It was the assistant director of the museum calling.

"I'm calling about Sherelle. Sherelle Aviv."

"You mean Sara Aviv, don't you?" Mrs. Doresh asked hesitantly.

"We call her Sherelle here at the museum," the man replied. "She said that's what her friends in Israel call her. You *are* Mrs. Doresh, aren't you?"

"Yes, this is she. Is there anything wrong?"

"Well—there was some trouble again today. The man who attacked her yesterday was back. He grabbed her arm. Made her drop a very valuable object she happened to be holding. And then he turned and ran away just like yesterday."

"But what—" By now, Mrs. Doresh was thoroughly alarmed.

"I think that this young lady needs protection. Right now, she's at the police station looking through the mug shot file—the pictures of holdup suspects, you know—but I understand that thus far they didn't come up with anyone. I suggest that you or your husband come down to the police station to pick her up and take her home."

*Three-cornered pastry

Mrs. Doresh immediately called her husband at the Yeshiva. *Rebbe* Doresh left at once for the police station. Sara was pale and shaken but in control of herself.

The family was ready to go to the synagogue, but Sara was not sure that she wanted to join them. "I'm not religious," she said. "I don't live in the past. You celebrate Purim because Haman, who tried to destroy the Jewish people, was exposed and hanged. But there are still plenty of evil characters around who would like to see Israel destroyed. When all those enemies are destroyed like Haman, then maybe I'll go to the synagogue also."

Devora tried to change Sara's mind, but this time Sara did not give in. "I'm afraid I couldn't go with you even if I wanted to," she said. "Somebody from the museum will be coming here tonight. He's bringing the slides he took of the objects I was holding yesterday and the ones I was holding today when the man attacked me again. You see, yesterday we were taking pictures of weapons; that might explain why the man shouted 'Murderer!' at me then. But the pictures we were taking today had nothing to do with weapons—no objects that had to do with killing, or with war. And yet the man came back and attacked me a second time. Now why should this poor old man have tried twice to harm me? He didn't look like a criminal. The photographer from the museum has a hunch of his own. He said that maybe the objects I was holding for the photographer today reminded the man of the weapons I'd been holding yesterday. He wants to show me the two sets of pictures so I can compare them and see whether I have any ideas. Maybe there were similarities in the design of the objects. . . ."

"Did the man say anything to you today?" Devora asked. "Did he call you 'murderer' again?"

"No, not this time," Sara replied. "And that's what's so strange. This time he shouted at me 'KGB!'"

"KGB? What's that?"

"It's the Russian secret police. In a way it is similer to Hitler's Gestapo. I know that I was born in Russia, but I left Russia when I was a very young child. I don't know why anyone looking at me should think of the KGB."

Devora was looking intently at Sara. "When did you arrive in Israel?" she asked.

"It's a long story," Sara began. "As I told you, I left Russia when I was very young, less than five years old. And you may think it strange, but I remember nothing about my life before I arrived in Israel. I must have blocked it out from my memory. All I know is that I was brought to Israel by an Israeli man and woman. Today I know they were members of a group that worked with an underground cell of Jews in Russia. I remember landing in Israel at night—by boat. But nothing about what happened before. It is as if a shade covered that part of my memory. Would you believe that I wasn't even sure of my own first name when I first arrived in Israel?"

Devora shook her head. "But—how did you get the name Sara?"

"I chose it because of this ring." Sara drew a gold ring from her finger, and handed it to Devora.

"What an unusual design!" Devora exclaimed. "I've never seen one like it!"

"It is all I have left from my early childhood," said Sara. "I had it on my finger when I left Russia. And I had the ring made bigger to fit my finger as I grew."

Devora looked closely at the design of the ring. She picked out an intricate pattern of Hebrew letters. "She—re—le," she read.

"What—?"

"The people who brought me to Israel explained to me that my name was Sherelle," Sara went on. "But that doesn't sound very Israeli, but I also knew that it's not a Russian name. So I changed it to Sara." She held out her hand. "I think you'd better go now, Devora. Your parents are waiting for you." Devora placed the ring into Sara's palm, and Sara slipped it back onto her finger.

For the first time in her life, Devora had trouble keeping her mind on the *Megillah** reading in the synagogue. Mrs. Doresh noticed it.

"What's the matter with you Devora?" she whispered when it was over. "You look as if you were a million miles away."

"Oh—er—nothing, Mother," Devora replied, embarrassed. She leaned forward in her seat and looked

*Scroll of Esther

down intently at the Megillah in her hands and kissed the words. She had tried to concentrate on the words of the story of Purim but she could not block out from her mind what Sara had told her. Sara had come to Israel from Russia . . . and all that she had left from her days in Russia was a gold ring with a most unusual design. . . . She—rel—le. . . .

When the family returned from the synagogue, Sara Aviv was waiting.

"Did the photographer come?" Devora asked.

"Yes, he did. Would you like to see the pictures, Devora? He left them here for me to study."

Devora studied the pictures with Sara. "Yes, there is one similarity between the pictures that were taken yesterday and those that your photographer took to-day," she said after a while. "But it is not in the objects you are holding up for the photographer. Look! Both sets show your right hand holding the objects. And see, there's the ring on your third finger. It shows up quite clearly."

"My ring? So—"

"Your ring does have a very unusual design, Sara. It's sufficiently unusual and large enough, to attract attention." Her eyes brightened, and grew large. "It wasn't the objects you were holding! It was probably the ring that caught the man's eyes! He saw it yester-day, and it made him come back today. . . ."

"I think it's time for Devora to go to bed." Mrs. Doresh had entered the room with her husband.

"There's *shul* early tomorrow, and then she has to help me prepare the Purim dinner. . . ."

"I've invited Mr. Cohen for our Purim dinner," *Rebbe* Doresh added. "He looks very sad. Perhaps going out and being with his friends will cheer him up a little."

The next morning Chaim and his friend Shimon went out to deliver *shalach monoth*, packages of Purim goodies, to their neighbors and friends. Chaim was dressed as a clown; Shimon wore a monkey costume.

By the late afternoon, the family was ready to sit down to their Purim dinner. Sara had come home early from the museum. "I didn't want to keep you waiting," she said to Mrs. Doresh. But Mr. Cohen had not yet arrived.

"I wonder what's keeping Mr. Cohen?" *Rebbe* Doresh said.

"We were at his house two hours ago to bring him his Purim package, but no one answered the door," said Chaim.

"He told me last night that he wasn't going to go to work today. With *shul* in the morning and the early dinner in the afternoon," *Rebbe* Doresh continued. "So where could he possibly be?"

Rebbe Doresh decided to go to Mr. Cohen's house himself to see what was the matter. The family sat down in the living room to wait for his return.

"I've got a Purim riddle for you," Chaim said. "Did you know how Haman got his name?" Since no one replied, Chaim answered his own question. "Well, it's an abbreviation. He's named for three other dictators who hated the Jews: *H* stands for Hitler, *M* stands for Hitler's friend Mussolini and *N* stands for Nasser in Egypt, whom the Jews beat in six days."

Sara Aviv smiled. "Yes, the Hebrew language is great for abbreviations. I remember going to a religious school in Israel, where they made us memorize the Ten Plagues. They taught us the three words made up by Rabbi Judah to help him remember the order in which the plagues came. *D'tzach, Adash, B'Achav.* Each of the consonants stood for one of the Ten Plagues."

"You're a little early, Sara," said Chaim. "It's still four weeks to go till Passover."

Devora frowned, then her whole face lit up. "I think I've solved our riddle!" she exclaimed.

"What? The Purim riddle? Kind of late, you know," Chaim teased.

Devora shook her head and smiled. "I mean the mystery of the man who attacked Sara at the museum."

"What's that have to do with what we've been talking about?" Chaim demanded.

"Sherelle! Sara's name back in Russia, which is part of the design on her ring! Sure, Sherelle is not an Israeli name—and not a Russian name either. It's an abbreviation—for the names of the four mothers of the Bible— *Sh* for Sarah, *R* for Rebecca and Rachel, and *L* for Leah."

Mrs. Doresh gasped. "Do you know what you just said?" she asked Devora.

"Sure I do," Devora cried. "I remember it all. . . .

Mr. Cohen—at the *shiva!* Remember the four rings he talked about?" Then she turned to Sara. "You say that the man who walked up to you and called you 'murderer' and 'KGB' was an older man? Say, in his sixties? And he needed a shave?"

"Yes, I'd say so," Sara replied.

An old man and unshaven! When Jews mourn a close relation, they let their beards grow. Now Devora was sure of herself.

The doorbell rang. Mr. Cohen entered, followed by *Rebbe* Doresh. "See, I was able to prevail on our friend to join us for the Purim dinner after all," *Rebbe* Doresh said happily.

Devora went up to her father and put her hand on his arm. "*Abba,* can we go into the kitchen? There's something I have to tell you."

When Devora and *Rebbe* Doresh returned to the living room, they both smiled at Mr. Cohen.

"G-d has His own way of solving mysteries and working wonders," he said. "Where's Miss Aviv?"

"She's in the kitchen, checking the meat," said Mrs. Doresh. "But I'll call her. She's been such a help, you have no idea. . . ."

Sara came into the living room. "Mr. Cohen," said *Rebbe* Doresh, "this is Miss Sara Aviv. She's our guest from Israel. But she was born in Russia. . . ."

Mr. Cohen was staring at Sara's face. His own face had turned white. "You—you here? So you weren't at the museum today any more—" His words ended in a hoarse whisper.

At the museum! Devora thought. So that's why

Chaim and his friend hadn't found Mr. Cohen at home! He'd been at the museum looking for the girl with the ring!

"May we see your ring?" *Rebbe* Doresh said to Sara gently. Sara took off the ring, and handed it to *Rebbe* Doresh, who in turn passed it to Mr. Cohen.

"Yes, yes, the ring!" Mr. Cohen cried. "How did you get to take my child's ring? It belonged to one of my daughters! What do you know about my daughters? Who killed them?"

Rebbe Doresh placed his hands on Mr. Cohen's shoulders and led him to the sofa. "Mr. Cohen, try to be calm," he said to him. "You have seen much sorrow, but now a wonderful thing has happened to you. This young lady—couldn't she be—"

"Sara! Sarale—my daughter!" Mr. Cohen leaped from the sofa and took Sara in his arms. *Rebbe* Doresh and his wife tiptoed out of the living room. Devora and Chaim followed without a word.

In the kitchen, Devora blew her nose hard. "Morah Hartman *was* right! Miracles didn't just happen thousands of years ago. They're still happening, all the time!"

"They certainly do," said Mrs. Doresh.

She quickly bent over the oven door, and removed the roast. "It'll be a miracle if that roast hasn't burned yet!" There was a little tremor in her voice. Then she straightened up and wiped her eyes with the corner of her apron. "Go inside, my little mystery solver," she said to Devora, "and finish setting the table."

The Shabbos Guest

W e're having company this Shabbos," *Rebbe* Doresh announced at the dinner table one Thursday evening in December. "I got a letter from my Yeshiva roomate, Sidney K⌐tz in Wilmington. His son Joshua will be here tomorrow morning."

Chaim clapped his hands. Whenever Josh came to the Doresh's to visit, Chaim had a good time. Joshua loved to play jokes and tricks, although he was almost 19 years old. *Rebbe* Doresh called Josh a *narrish kop*, a young fool. Devora frowned. She wasn't exactly looking forward to Josh's visit because she always ended up as the victim of his jokes.

"Is there any particular reason why he's coming?" her mother asked.

Rebbe Doresh pulled a letter from his pocket. "This is what Sidney writes, 'Tomorrow is Joshua's birthday. He will be 19 years old. . . . He's entitled to some inheritance money which was set aside for him by his mother's parents, the Rubins.'" *Rebbe* Doresh folded the letter. "Poor Sidney," he said. "He's been sick for years. He's in a wheelchair all the time now. His wife took a job to pay some of the bills. Her parents, the

Rubins, were never happy that she married Sidney. She was their only daughter and they had wanted her to marry a wealthy businessman, not a teacher. But the Rubins loved Josh. He was their only grandchild and they wanted him to have enough money to get along for the rest of his life, even without working."

"Yeah, that's a good idea," Chaim cut in. "I guess Josh isn't exactly brilliant."

"No *loshen ho-ra,** young man," *Rebbe* Doresh said sternly. "Anyway, to continue the story. Josh's grandparents arranged things so that he should get the money piecemeal, not all at once. Part of the money comes to him now, on his nineteenth birthday. He'll get the next part when he's 25, another when he's 30, and so forth, until he has it all."

"I'm happy for Josh," said Mrs. Doresh. "I just hope he doesn't fritter it all away on foolishness."

Chaim slurped up his milk through his straw. "If Josh gets so much money, do you think I could talk him into buying me an encyclopedia?" he asked.

Devora coughed. "I always thought you wanted a chemistry set."

"Enough of this silly talk," said *Rebbe* Doresh. "The money belongs to Josh, and you are not to ask him for any presents."

After the children had *benshed*** and left the table to

*Derogatory or damaging speech
**Said the Grace after meals

do their homework, *Rebbe* Doresh said to his wife in a low voice, "As a matter of fact, Josh's father is very worried about him. Josh was never very smart, you know, and he has a tendency to hook up to the wrong ideas and the wrong people. His father is afraid that he'll go around bragging about his inheritance, and somebody will take advantage of him. Sidney hopes that I'll be able to talk some sense into the boy."

"That'll be no easy matter, I'm afraid," Mrs. Doresh sighed. "Josh, as you know, can be quite stubborn when he makes up his mind to do something. Do you remember that crazy invention of his—the permanent handkerchief?"

Rebbe Doresh began to laugh. "Do I remember? He ruined two of my best handkerchiefs trying to demonstrate his invention. He sewed two handkerchiefs together and cut a large round hole in the middle. He put a piece of Kleenex in between the two handkerchiefs. It filled up the hole. You were supposed to blow your nose just into the Kleenex, and then throw the piece of Kleenex away. Put in a new piece of Kleenex and—presto—you had a fresh, clean handkerchief without having to go through the trouble of washing it."

Now Mrs. Doresh was laughing too. "And he kept making the handkerchiefs by the hundreds, until his parents stopped giving him money! Poor Josh! He's a good boy, but I wish he had more sense."

Josh didn't turn up at the Doresh home until after

two o'clock Friday afternoon. The family had expected him in the morning, and it was winter time so that Shabbos would begin very early. But Josh's smile was so charming that no one felt like asking him why he was so late.

"I saw a lawyer today. Very, very important," Josh told *Rebbe* Doresh. He cleared his throat, pretended to put on eyeglasses, bent forward and pursed his lips. "Mister Katz," he imitated the lawyer, "as the party of the first part you are entitled to the first part." Then he rubbed his hands together and laughed. "I had no idea that Grandpa Rubin thought that much of me." He opened his little suitcase and handed Mrs. Doresh a small box. "For you, madam," he said with an elegant bow.

Mrs. Doresh opened the box and gasped. Inside, resting on a flimsy piece of cotton, was the gaudiest necklace she had ever seen. Josh had obviously spent a lot of money for it, but it was also clear that he still had a lot to learn about good taste.

"I like you, Mrs. Doresh," said Josh modestly, "so I thought I'd give you something I like."

"Really, Josh, you shouldn't have. . ." Mrs. Doresh was a little upset. She did not want to hurt the young man's feelings.

Chaim had come into the kitchen. "What's this?" he asked, seeing the box in his mother's hand. "Sure looks horrible."

Mrs. Doresh gave her son a special warning look,

and he stopped talking. But Josh did not seem to have heard Chaim.

"You mustn't think I'd forget about you, young man," Josh said, handing Chaim a large box. "I remember you once said you'd like a chemistry set, so here it is."

Chaim was so surprised that he didn't say a word.

"Well, I hope I made the right choice," Josh continued. "Now, where's Devora?"

Chaim had gotten his voice back. "She's upstairs preparing herself for one of your tricks," he said, and grinned.

Again, Mrs. Doresh shook her head at her son. "Devora'll be down in a minute," she said.

When Devora came downstairs, Josh had a necklace for her also. Then he handed *Rebbe* Doresh his gift—a pipe. "I know you don't smoke, *Rebbe* Doresh, but just holding a pipe adds to a man's look of intelligence," he said laughing at his own joke.

Rebbe Doresh sighed. "None of this was really necessary, Josh."

"Why not? Whenever I come to New York, I stay at your house, and you're always putting yourselves out for me. So this is just a small token of appreciation. You know, when you get into the business world, you have to show your friends that you appreciate what they do for you."

Later, *Rebbe* Doresh sat down with Josh in the den.

"You know, *Rebbe*, I have some great plans in mind

about what to do with the money. And if things come through the way I expect, I'll be a really wealthy man."

Rebbe Doresh sighed, but said nothing.

As he walked out of the den, Josh saw Devora sitting at the dinner room table studying. "What are you reading?" he asked her.

"About somebody who has the same name as you," Devora replied. "Joshua, who took over as leader of the Children of Israel after Moses died."

"My dear young lady, just because I've dropped out of the Yeshiva doesn't mean I forgot my Bible," Josh retorted. "But why does Joshua interest you so?"

"I was studying Chapter 10 of the Book of Joshua, where Joshua ordered the sun not to set so the Children of Israel would be able to continue their battle in daylight and defeat their enemies."

"Well, sometimes I wouldn't mind if my days would be longer," said Josh. "Then I'd have more time for my business affairs." He sat down on one of the chairs near the dining room table and moved closer to Devora. "For instance," he began, "I have this extremely important deal to complete. The problem is that I can't finish it until tonight. My contact man is in Florida, and he's out all day, working. I can reach him only after work, which is about an hour before Shabbos begins. I sent word to him to go straight home after work today because I wanted to call him at home before Shabbos. But I'm not happy with this arrangement because we really would need more time to finish everything."

"What kind of deal is it that can't wait until tomorrow night?" Devora asked, making it sound as if she really wasn't particularly interested in finding out.

Josh sat up tall in his chair. "A very important deal," he said. He looked around the room, then continued in a stage whisper. "It's real high finance. The other day I had to go to Philadelphia. Well, on the train, I met a man who told me about some stock certificates he and a friend of his wanted to sell. At a real bargain price, too!"

"So why did he have to tell you about them?" Devora asked. "Why didn't he go to a stockbroker? Isn't the stockbroker the one who sells stocks for people?"

Josh smiled. "Silly girl," he said. "If he went to a broker, he couldn't sell the certificates so cheaply, because he'd have to pay the broker."

"But I don't get it," Devora persisted. "This man never saw you before. Why did he pick you, of all the people on the train?"

Josh pulled a pipe from his shirt pocket and put it into his mouth. "I was sitting there just like this, with the pipe in my mouth. He said I looked like an intelligent man, and perhaps I would like to earn some money."

Devora looked at him in surprise. "So he thought he could tell from the way you looked that you were smart?"

"Yes," Josh nodded proudly. "That's why I gave your father a pipe, too. He'll find that people will

notice him when he has it in his hand or in his mouth."
Then he continued. "Mr. Gold—that's the man I met
on the train—Mr. Gold has a partner, Mr. Saulson, who
wanted to sell the certificates to a man he knew in New
York. But Mr. Gold doesn't like that man in New
York. He told me he didn't trust him. He said he'd
prefer to sell to somebody else and, if I'd be willing to
buy the certificates for the same price. . . ."

"Did you see the certificates?" Devora asked.

"Sure I did. Mr. Gold happened to have one of them
on him. I never agree to buy anything until I've had a
good look at it first. He really was going to give me a
very good deal. I told him I was interested and that I
was going to New York in a few days to withdraw
some money."

"Have you asked anyone else about this? Maybe
someone at a bank?"

"No, I didn't. And, Devora, I don't want you to
blab to your father about this either. It's my money and
I know that it's a good investment."

"But you don't know anything about this Mr. Gold,
Josh. How do you know you can trust him?"

"Well, for heaven's sake, he's Jewish, isn't he? Do
you mean Jewish people shouldn't trust each other?"

Devora frowned. The whole story didn't seem right
to her.

"Did you buy the certificates already?" she asked.

"No, of course not, silly. I had to make sure first
that I had access to the money from my grandparents.
Well, I checked that out here today. Then I contacted

Mr. Gold's office. His secretary gave me the number to call in Florida—it's Mr. Gold's partner."

"So when will you call this man in Florida?"

"Before Shabbos. As soon as he gets home from work. I'll tell him that I'm ready to make the deal. He'll fly in sometime tomorrow, and we'll sign tomorrow night."

"Mr. Gold's partner's coming in tomorrow? Shabbos?"

"So what? Mr. Saulson's not religious. Neither is Mr. Gold. But they know I am *frum*.* So they're willing to wait until tomorrow night to sign the deal, as long as I gave my OK on Friday. Now if Shabbos would start just a little later . . ."

Rebbe Doresh poked his head into the dining room. "You'd better hurry and get ready," he told Josh and Devora. "Shabbos begins in an hour's time."

"What time is it now?" Josh asked.

"It's 3:15. Shabbos will begin at 4:15. Winter time, you know. It gets dark very early."

"Would you mind if I make a long distance call, *Rebbe* Doresh?" Josh asked. "I'll pay for it, of course."

Rebbe Doresh nodded and smiled. "Don't worry about it. Be my guest." He pointed to the phone in the kitchen.

Joshua went into the kitchen. Devora began to set the dining room table for Shabbos dinner.

"What was he talking to you about?" her father asked.

"A business deal of his," Devora replied. "He said I

*Observant

wasn't supposed to tell you about it. But I don't like this. Something's wrong."

Just then Josh returned to the dining room. "I guess the man hasn't come home from work yet."

"What man?" *Rebbe* Doresh asked.

Josh sat down and drummed his fingers on the dining room table as Devora brought in the plates.

"Did you tell your father about this?" he asked her angrily.

Devora shook her head. *Rebbe* Doresh sat down beside Josh. "Look, I can't stop you from doing whatever you want. . . . Besides, it's just before Shabbos. So what could I do anyway?"

"Oh, you might as well know, *Rebbe* Doresh. I agreed with a Mr. Saulson in Florida that I would call him today, one hour before Shabbos begins."

"What about?" *Rebbe* Doresh asked.

"I want to buy some stock certificates from him," Josh replied.

"Why all the hurry? Can't it wait till after Shabbos?"

Josh stood up angrily. "Why should it? It's a very good deal, I tell you."

Rebbe Doresh tried to quiet him down. "If it's really such a good deal, then Mr. Saulson ought to be home any minute, waiting for your call. Tell me, Josh— is this Mr. Saulson religious?"

"No, he isn't. But what difference does that make? He knows when Shabbos begins. Even Mr. Gold knows that." He walked back toward the kitchen.

Devora and her father looked at each other.

"What don't you like about that deal Joshua was telling you about?" he asked her in a low voice.

"Just about everything, *Abba*."

Joshua was back in the dining room. "I'll give him another five minutes," he said.

"Could I buy into your deal?" *Rebbe* Doresh asked him.

Joshua gave *Rebbe* Doresh a surprised look. "Oh, I forgot. My father once told me that you know something about investments. Well, if you do, then I'm sure you will understand why I don't want to talk about it right now. Now—if you'll excuse me. . . ." With that, he turned and went up the stairs to the room where he always stayed when he came to the Doresh home.

"This is going to spoil our entire Shabbos," *Rebbe* Doresh said to Devora. Every few minutes, for the rest of that hour, Josh tried calling Mr. Saulson in Florida, but no one answered. Finally, moments before he and *Rebbe* Doresh left the house to go to shul, Josh slammed the receiver down for the last time.

"Did you ever hear such a thing?" he demanded. "I sent him word to be home an hour before Shabbos. Mr. Gold promised me that he would. I said I was going to call him an hour before Shabbos. And he isn't home yet! It's 4:15 and he still isn't home!"

Mrs. Doresh had come to the door. "Well, if this gentleman, whoever he is, isn't religious, it would be quite early for him to go home from work," she volunteered.

"Look, *Rebbe* Doresh," said Joshua. "You go on to shul and I'll keep trying Florida. I'll follow you as soon as I've talked to Mr. Saulson. You see, there's someone else who wants to buy the certificates and I want to beat him to it."

"I'm sorry, Josh," *Rebbe* Doresh said sternly. "We do not do business in this house after the Sabbath begins. You cannot make phone calls from here on Shabbos."

Joshua's face was flushed. "Well, then I'll go someplace else to do it," he said.

"I'd really prefer that you don't break the Shabbos, especially not when you're a guest in my house. Come on, let's go to shul."

Joshua put down the receiver. "Because of Shabbos, I'll lose out on this deal," he said to himself as he and *Rebbe* Doresh walked out of the house.

While the men were away at shul, the Doresh phone rang several times. Devora looked at her mother nervously. Her mother shook her head. "Don't say anything about it to him, Devora. Or else when he comes back, he'll run to the phone if it rings again."

When the men returned from shul, Joshua was still in a dark mood. "I can't understand it," he muttered. "He promised me he'd be waiting at the phone for my call, one hour before Shabbos. What do you think could have happened?"

The family sang *z'miroth** as usual at the table, but Josh did not join in the singing. After the meal and the *benshing* had ended, Joshua still sat in his chair, staring down at the white Shabbos tablecloth. Devora felt sorry for him.

"Can I tell you a story, Josh?" she began. "You probably heard it long ago, but anyway. . . It's about Rabbi Nahum who was called '*Gam Zu*' because whenever anything bad or unpleasant happened to him, he would say, '*Gam Zu Le-Tovah*'—'even this is for the good.' One day the Jews in ancient Israel decided to send a gift to the emperor of Rome so that he would not wage war against them. They chose a chest filled with diamonds and other precious stones. It was decided that Rabbi Nahum should be asked to take the gift to Rome personally to present to the emperor. It was a long journey, so Rabbi Nahum stopped at an inn for the night. While he was asleep the inkeeper crept into his room, opened the chest, took out all the jewelry, and filled the empty chest with dirt before he closed it again. The next morning, Rabbi Nahum took the chest and continued on his way. When he arrived at the emperor's palace, he presented the chest to the emperor. When the emperor opened the chest and saw that it was full of dirt, he was furious and wanted to kill Rabbi Nahum. But one of the guards said to him, 'Look at this man, Your Majesty, how he stands there with no fear in his eyes. It must be that what is in this chest is not dirt

*Sabbath songs

but some kind of magic sand. That's why he isn't afraid of you, or of anyone else here.' At that moment, Rabbi Nahum said aloud, 'Gam Zu Le-Tovah.' The Romans tossed the dirt into the air, and the pieces of dirt turned into arrows, which killed all of the emperor's enemies. The emperor was so pleased that he gave Rabbi Nahum a whole truckful of precious stones as a reward. Rabbi Nahum thanked him, and said again, 'Gam Zu Le-Tovah.' What had looked like a piece of bad luck had turned into something very good for him. Maybe Josh, that's the way you should feel about Mr. Saulson. Perhaps the fact that they didn't answer your call may bring you something good."

"How could anything good come from that?" Josh asked, annoyed. "Maybe I should have forgotten about Shabbos, just this one time. *That* might have brought me something good."

The next day, after the Sabbath had ended, Josh tried to call Miami again. But again the phone rang and rang and rang, without an answer. "I don't understand it," he said, over and over again. "I could have made a mint from those certificates and on account of Shabbos somebody else beat me to the deal." He put on his coat. "I'm going to buy a newspaper," he told Mrs. Doresh. "Maybe the air'll help clear my head."

When he returned ten minutes later, his eyes were filled with shock and amazement. "Can you believe—" he sputtered. He handed the paper to *Rebbe* Doresh. *Rebbe* Doresh began to read aloud:

STOLEN STOCK CERTIFICATES RECOVERED

The police have announced the arrest here today of Sam Gold of Brooklyn, Robert Saulson of Miami, Florida, Sal Genovese, of Tampa, Florida, and Herbert Mil of Detroit, Michigan. All four were involved in a scheme to sell stolen stock certificates. They had come to New York and were caught because the last individual they had approached as a prospective customer happened to be an FBI informer. The men were taken to the 56th Precinct Station. . . .

"Is that . . . is that *your* Mr. Gold, Josh?" Devora asked.

Josh poured himself a glass of soda. His hands were shaking. "It sure is. . . . Can you beat that? Stolen stock certificates!"

"You're just lucky you never agreed to the deal," said Mrs. Doresh.

"But what I still don't understand," Josh persisted, "is why Saulson didn't answer my calls. After all, Mr. Saulson wasn't arrested in Florida last night, but only today, after he arrived in New York. So he still had plenty of time to receive my call. Well, Devora, whatever it was—it looks as if you were right. This sure was a case of *Gam Zu Le-Tovah*."

Devora smiled. "I'm afraid there's something more to this. You see, Mr. Saulson couldn't have been home in time to receive your call."

"Why not? I told him to be home and ready for my call one hour before Shabbos. He knew when Shabbos begins; besides, if he'd forgotten, he could always have looked in the newspaper for the hour of sunset."

"That's just it, Josh. Joshua in the Bible got the sun to stand still for him. For you, the sun didn't exactly stand still, but in Florida, you might say, it took its time about setting. You see, Florida is closer to the equator than New York, so Shabbos in Florida during the winter time starts exactly one hour later than it does here. In New York, Shabbos began at 4:15 yesterday, but in Miami it didn't start until 5:15."

"Are you sure, Devora?" Josh asked.

"Positive," Devora replied. "So, if you agreed with Mr. Saulson that you were going to call him one hour before Shabbos, Florida time, in Florida, one hour before Shabbos was not 3:15 like in New York, but 4:15, when it was already Shabbos here."

"Well," Chaim chimed in. "*Gam Zu Le-Tovah.* . . . It's lucky I have such a smart sister who knows all that, but now, if I could have an encyclopedia, then. . ." At a look from his father, he stopped himself.

Joshua shook his head. He hadn't heard Chaim at all. "*Rebbe* Doresh," he said. "I'm glad I was with you this Friday and that you stopped me from breaking the Sabbath. If you hadn't stopped me, I would have made that phone call, and I could have been in real trouble with the police. From now on, I'll be more careful about Shabbos—and about the people I do business with. Thanks to you, I've really learned my lesson."

Chaim had to have the last word. "*Gam Zu Le-Tovah,*" he yelled.

The Case of Pedigree Penina

haim Doresh, what have you done with my Hebrew dictionary?"

Devora stormed into the kitchen where Chaim was sitting with his milk and cookies.

"I haven't done anything with it. I haven't even touched it!" her brother shouted back.

Mrs. Doresh frowned. "Since when do my children shout at each other? Are you really sure your dictionary is missing, Devora?"

"I am not only positive that it is missing, but also that my dear brother borrowed it and forgot to bring it back." Devora glared at Chaim.

"I don't need your dictionary. I have my own," Chaim yelled.

"Then why did you borrow mine last week?" Devora asked.

Chaim grinned sheepishly. "Because I can't find my dictionary. . . . But I put yours back. Don't you remember? You were sitting in the living room with Shaindy and I showed you I had it in my hands and I was going to return it to your room."

"I remember," Devora agreed, "And the dictionary was on my shelf. But you must have borrowed it again today, because it isn't there any more. Who else in this house would want to take it?"

"Well, not I," Chaim retorted angrily. "I always get accused."

Mrs. Doresh sighed and looked at Devorah. "If Chaim says he didn't take it, then I don't think he'd tell you an untruth," she said.

"But all the evidence points to Chaim," Devora insisted. "He has a dictionary of his own, just like mine. He lost his, so last week he borrowed mine; and since his dictionary is still missing, he decided to borrow mine again today. It's as simple as that."

Mrs. Doresh shook her head. "But he says that when he borrowed it, he returned it. . . ."

"Well, Mother, who else could have taken it?" Devora demanded.

"Try to solve that mystery," Chaim advised, "and in the meantime, give me the benefit of the doubt." He sounded very grownup.

Mrs. Doresh nodded and smiled. "When you suspect someone of wrongdoing, give him the benefit of the doubt—*don l'kaf z'chus*—until you're sure. That's the Jewish way. Is it possible, Devora, that you yourself misplaced your dictionary?"

"I'm sure I didn't," Devora insisted. "And by the way, how do I know that Chaim didn't take my dictionary, to begin with. After all, both dictionaries are exactly the same. Maybe Chaim first lost his, and then mine."

"Are those the dictionaries your Uncle Pesach

brought you from Israel?" Mrs. Doresh asked. "They were beautiful soft-cover picture dictionaries, with Hebrew definitions, weren't they?"

"That's exactly why I need my dictionary now," said Devora. "I am writing a report on *Sukkot** for school. It's all in Hebrew."

Mrs. Doresh sighed. "Well, I suppose Chaim is right. . . . Another mystery for Devora to solve." With that, she pulled a memo pad from her purse and began to write. "I wouldn't know what I'd do if I lost my memo pad," she said, half to herself. "It's the only way I remember everything I have to do—shopping, meetings, appointments. . . . I check it every morning and every evening, and then I cross out the things I already did that day." She put the memo pad back into her purse. "There's still a lot of shopping I have to do for *Sukkot.*" She hung her purse onto her aluminum shopping cart, which was lined with a grey plastic bag, and which she always kept near the kitchen door, ready to use.

The doorbell rang. Devora went to the door.

It was the mailman, Mr. Sheinbaum. He smiled at Devora as he handed her the mail.

"Have you put up your *Sukkah* yet?" he asked.

Mr. Sheinbaum was not only the Doresh family's mailman but also their neighbor and friend. He lived in an apartment house across the street. Usually, he would eat in the Doresh *Sukkah* during *Hol HaMoed,* the

*Festival of Tabernacles

middle days of Sukkot. Unlike many other apartment
house owners in the neighborhood, Mr. Sheinbaum's
landlord did not permit his Jewish tenants to set up a
Sukkah on the roof. So the Sheinbaum family—Mr.
Sheinbaum, his wife and their little daughter, 2-year-
old Adelle, would spend the first two days of the holi-
day at the home of Mrs. Sheinbaum's parents in
Monsey, just north of New York City, where almost
every Jewish family had a *Sukkah,* and return to Brooklyn for the middle days, when Mr. Sheinbaum had to
go to work.

For the past two weeks, ever since *Rosh Hashanah,*
the Jewish New Year, one or the other of the Sheinbaums, with little Adelle toddling along, had been in
and out of the Doresh home almost every day to ask
when *Rebbe* Doresh would be ready to put up his
Sukkah. Since the Sheinbaums were going to eat in the
Doresh *Sukkah* for six days, they wanted to have a share
in the *Sukkah* by helping set it up.

As Mr. Sheinbaum turned to leave, he was startled
by a loud bark. A tall dark-haired man, with a trimmed
black beard and mustache was walking up to the
Doresh house. With him was a huge black and gray
dog. The dog's bark could be heard all the way down
the block. Some of the children who had been playing
on the sidewalk ran into their front yards and bolted the
gates behind them. They did not like this dog.

"Down, Esau, down!" said the man with the black
beard as Mr. Sheinbaum stood petrified. The big dog

stopped in his tracks and sniffed at Mr. Sheinbaum's shoes.

"You're lucky to get your mail this early in the day," the stranger said to Devora. "My mail doesn't come till late in the afternoon." Then he looked at Devora. "By the way, do you know a Miss Devora Doresh on this block?" he asked her. He had a foreign accent, which reminded Devora of one of her Israeli cousins.

"It happens that I know Miss Doresh," Devora cautiously replied, keeping her distance from the dog. "But who are you?"

"My name is Yaakov Kol," the stranger said. "I have a letter here from an Officer O'Malley, of the 56th precinct, suggesting that I look up Miss Doresh."

Devora turned her head. Her mother was now standing behind her in the doorway. "May I see the letter?" Mrs. Doresh asked. "This is the Doresh residence."

Mr. Sheinbaum moved a few steps away, but the dog barked again.

"Esau! Quiet!" Mr. Kol shouted.

"Esau! What an odd name for a dog," said Devora.

"I found him in an Egyptian army camp my outfit occupied during the Yom Kippur War. The Egyptians had fled and left him behind. That's why I call him Esau—because just like Esau in the Bible, he lived with the enemies of the Jews. And, as you can see, this dog isn't exactly friendly." Mr. Kol pushed back his right shirt sleeve. There was an ugly scar on his arm. "See, that's what Esau did to me the first time I tried to feed him."

Mr. Sheinbaum edged carefully away.

"Won't you come in, Mr. Kol?" Mrs. Doresh asked.

"Esau! Stay!" Mr. Kol commanded, then followed Devora and her mother into the house.

In the living room, Mrs. Doresh invited Mr. Kol to sit down. "As you have probably guessed by now, this young lady is my daughter, Miss Devora Doresh."

Mr. Kol looked at Mrs. Doresh, then at Devora. "Frankly, I didn't expect Miss Doresh to be such a young girl."

Mrs. Doresh ignored the remark. "But exactly what does Officer O'Malley want my daughter to do for you, Mr. Kol?"

"Well, I've received a number of threatening letters, but so far the threat in the letters hasn't been carried out. In short, no crime has been committed—not yet. So the police said there was nothing they could do for me. After all, you can't expect the police to provide 24-hour guard service for a dog just because someone has threatened to kidnap it. But I personally can't afford a private guard or detective service. So Officer O'Malley told me to come here, and here I am."

Devora looked at Mr. Kol in surprise. "You mean Esau needs—"

"No, it's not Esau who needs guard service," Mr.

Kol replied, laughing. "He usually travels with us. Let me explain. My family and I in Israel—we're dog breeders and trainers, and we've been doing very well lately. In the early days, people in Israel didn't have enough money, or food, for that matter, to keep a dog, except maybe as guard dogs in a kibbutz. But now most Israelis have a little money, so they enjoy keeping dogs as pets. And when they buy a dog, they demand the very best. You have no idea how choosy they've become about such things as pedigree."

Chaim had joined his mother and sister in the living room. "So in what language do you talk to your dogs?" he asked. "How do you give them your commands? All in Hebrew?"

"Yes, in Hebrew, but also in English and sometimes even in German. It all depends on where I bought that particular dog, and what language it was taught to understand before I bought it. The German is for German shepherd dogs. They usually get their first training in Germany. They're mostly used as watch dogs."

"Why did you leave Israel?" Chaim inquired.

"I didn't leave. We—my assistant and I—are only here for a visit. We want to buy some pedigree dogs here and take them back with us to Israel to train and sell. We go to all sorts of foreign countries to buy unusual dogs. And we'll be glad to get back to Israel because then we'll have the dogs safe in proper cages. Here, in our makeshift quarters, there's always the danger that they might be stolen. Now just two weeks ago, we were lucky enough to get a chihuahua. This is a tiny breed, very rare, and very expensive. I'm really proud of the little lady, and so is Mordecai."

"Mordecai? Who is he?" Chaim asked.

"That's my assistant. And he's part of my problem. Mordecai was originally an American. He moved to Israel about eight years ago. I hired him on the spot, because I saw immediately that he had a way with animals. But unfortunately, it looks as if I made a mistake."

"Do you mean that Mordecai isn't working out?" Devora asked.

"It's a little more complicated than that, I'm afraid. I'm staying at a nice apartment house in this neighborhood. We're planning to stay here at least six months, so a hotel would be too expensive. Besides, I wanted to live in a Jewish section. Now just this week, I found out that Mordecai got himself an American girl friend. It turns out that the girl's parents are also in the dog business. What's more, they're living in the same apartment house as Mordecai and I."

"So Mordecai told you—" Mrs. Doresh inquired.

"No, Mrs. Doresh, that's just the trouble. He didn't tell me himself. I learned about it in the street, by accident. In this neighborhood everybody seems to know about everybody else, just like back home in my section of Jerusalem."

"Well, so Mordecai has a girl friend with parents in the same business as you, Mr. Kol, and Mordecai never told you about it," said Devora. "But is that any reason for suspecting that Mordecai—Do you mean you're afraid Mordecai intends to steal that chihuahua from you and take it to his girl friend's parents?"

Mr. Kol looked straight into Devora's face. "Yes, I am." He thrust his hand into his coat pocket, and pulled out a packet of letters, which he handed to Devora. "Every day for the past two weeks I have been receiving threatening letters. They say that someone is out to kidnap my chihuahua. I am convinced that it was Mordecai who started it all. I don't feel I can trust him any more. And I can't stay home and watch that little dog all the time."

Devora examined the envelopes. "How did you get these letters?" she asked. "They have no postmark on them. So it couldn't have come to you in the mail." Mr. Kol nodded. "The letters get slipped under my door. But when I run to the door, nobody is there, and I can't see anyone leaving the building. So the letters must come from someone living inside the house. You see, everything points to Mordecai and his girl friend's family."

There was a scream from outside. Mrs. Doresh rushed to the door. Chaim came in, carrying Adelle, Mr. Sheinbaum's daughter. The little girl was howling, but obviously not hurt. "She must have gone through the back yard," said Chaim, "and around to the front. Esau didn't do anything to her; he just scared her."

Devora nodded and looked at Mr. Kol. "And you feel quite sure it's Mordecai, do you?" she asked. "Or do you still have some doubts?"

"I'd like to be wrong about Mordecai," Mr. Kol replied."But I'm afraid that. . . ."

Mrs. Doresh nodded. "You think he deliberately didn't tell you about his girl friend's parents and this bothers you. But I think you'd rather give him the benefit of the doubt, wouldn't you? *Don l'kaf z'chus—* that's the Jewish way."

Mr. Kol turned to Devora. "I'd like you to come with me to see my apartment and the chihuahua. Perhaps you'll be able to find some clue as to where these letters might be coming from and how these people— whoever they are—might be planning to kidnap the animal."

"All right, Devora," her mother said. "You may go with Mr. Kol."

"By the way," said Mr. Kol, smiling. "I gave my chihuahua an unofficial name—half English, half Hebrew. I'm calling her Pedigree Penina."

Chaim laughed aloud. "Pedigree Penina," he began to sing to little Adelle Sheinbaum, who had stopped crying and was giving Chaim a big smile.

"My car is just down the block," Mr. Kol said to Devora. "I wasn't sure which of the houses was yours, so I parked at the corner and walked up the block to check the house numbers." Esau, restrained by a metal chain, trotted ahead of his master.

The bells from a nearby church rang the noon hour as Mr. Kol parked his car in front of the building where he had rented his apartment. Just as he was about to ring the bell, the front door of the house was opened by a young man. Devora liked the way the young man looked. He had an honest face. "This is my assistant, Mordecai," said Mr. Kol. Devora felt embarrassed. After hearing Mr. Kol's story, she, too, had been inclined to think of Mordecai as the most obvious suspect, but there was something about Mordecai that made her feel she had been too hasty in her judgment. True, her father had often warned her, "Do not judge a book by its cover," but she could not help feeling that Mordecai simply did not look like an untrustworthy character.

"Where's Penina?" Mr. Kol asked Mordecai.

"She's upstairs. I just came down for two minutes, to get the mail. It came early today, for a change. I wish we had Mr. Sheinbaum. Then we'd get our mail early all the time." Mordecai handed Mr. Kol a few letters. One of them was not postmarked. Mr. Kol passed it to Devora. The letter consisted of one sheet with only one word. That word was "Soon."

Mr. Kol, Mordecai and Devora went up the stairs. Mr. Kol's apartment was on the third floor. When they opened the apartment door, Mr. Kol's face turned white. The front room looked as if a tornado had struck it. As for Penina, she was nowhere to be found.

"My God!" Mordecai exclaimed. "I was gone only two minutes! How could anybody have gotten into the place in that short time?"

Mr. Kol grabbed Mordecai by the collar. "Why did you ever leave that dog alone in the apartment, when I told you she mustn't be left for even a second? Just tell me why!"

The window was open wide, but there was no fire escape which the intruders could have used to make a quick getaway. But next to the window, Devora smelled a strange odor. She sniffed and traced the smell to a white cloth on the floor near the window. She picked up the cloth. "What's this?" she said.

Mordecai took the cloth from Devora and sniffed it. "It's ether."

"Ether!" Mr. Kol shouted. "Well, that's a nice mess. Somebody broke into this place, put the rag over Penina's mouth so she should go to sleep and not bark her head off, and took her out of the house. She's small enough to fit into a shopping bag."

A shopping bag. . . . Devora was still standing by the window, looking out into the street below.

"Quick!" she shouted. "Mr. Kol! There's the mailman leaving the house! His bag . . . Run, somebody! Stop him!"

Mr. Kol and Mordecai rushed out the door, with Esau running after them. From the window, Devora saw the mailman break into a run, but Esau caught up with him quickly, grabbed him by the pants and held him until Mr. Kol could get at him. While Mr. Kol and Esau held the mailman, Mordecai removed the pouch from the mailman's shoulder and opened it. Sure enough, Penina was inside, fast asleep but otherwise unhurt.

Devora, upstairs, phoned the police. Minutes later, a police car pulled up in front of the house and Officer O'Malley got out. After a few words with Mr. Kol and Mordecai, Officer O'Malley handcuffed the mailman and ordered him to get into the car.

By the time Devora came outside, the police car with Officer O'Malley and the mailman had gone.

"How did you ever suspect the mailman, Devora?" Mr. Kol asked.

"Simple," Devora replied modestly. "This morning, at our house, you happened to mention that your mailman only comes to your house late in the afternoon. But today he came much earlier. Remember, when Mordecai opened the door for us, the church bells had just struck twelve. Never mind that the threatening letters you kept getting weren't postmarked. The mailman could have slipped them under your door anytime. The important thing was that today, of all days, he came at an unusually early hour, when he knew you wouldn't be expecting him and might even be out of the house. Mordecai was out of the apartment for only two minutes, just when the mailman was in the house. This was perfect timing for the mailman; he handed the mail to Mordecai, then went right past him into the building. Nobody could suspect a mailman for going past the mailboxes into an apartment house. After all, there are some envelopes and packages that are too big for the mailboxes, so the mailman has to deliver them personally. Except, in this case, he didn't go into the house to deliver a package, but to take Penina. And then, just as I saw the mailman leave, Mr. Kol happened to say that Penina was small enough to fit into a shopping bag. . . . It occurred to me that a mailman's pouch is an even better place than a shopping bag for hiding a dog of Penina's size."

At supper that evening, Devora told her parents the story. The mailman had admitted that he had written the letters and taken the dog. He lived all alone, he told the police, and had always wanted a dog to keep him company, but his apartment was too small for a big animal.

"So he thought a tiny dog like Penina would be just right," said *Rebbe* Doresh. "It looks to me like that poor man was a little crazy or not very bright—or maybe both."

"And what about Mordecai?" Mrs. Doresh asked. "Is he going to stay on as Mr. Kol's assistant?"

"He certainly is, Mother," Devora replied. "What's more, Mr. Kol intends to meet his girl friend's parents, and maybe they'll be doing business together in the future."

"And Mr. Kol was all ready to believe the worst of Mordecai, just because he didn't tell him that his girl friend's parents were dog breeders, too," said Mrs. Doresh. "Do you see now how important it is to give everyone the benefit of the doubt before accusing him of wrongdoing? If Mr. Kol would have accused Mordecai to his face, Mordecai would probably have quit on the spot and Mr. Kol would have lost a good and reliable assistant."

"Speaking of losing things, I have an announcement to make," Chaim interrupted.

"Devora and I didn't misplace our dictionaries. I think I know who did."

"Well, Chaim, don't keep us in suspense," said Devora.

"It was that little monkey, Adelle. Every time she tags along after her parents to find out how our *Sukkah* is getting along, she heads straight for the bookshelves. Today I saw her do it again. I'll bet she's the one who took the dictionaries."

"So where do you think she put them?" Devora asked.

"I don't know," Chaim answered. "Adelle talks a mile a minute, but who can understand what she's saying?"

"While you're figuring out that mystery, Devora," Mrs. Doresh suggested, "why don't you go out into the kitchen and bring in the dessert?"

Devora walked to the kitchen door, "Oops!" she exclaimed. "I almost tripped over Mother's shopping cart." She bent over the aluminum cart, with its gray plastic lining. "Look at that!" She reached into the cart and pulled out two little books. "Our Hebrew dictionaries! Adelle must have thrown them into the shopping cart!"

"It seems to be her favorite place for throwing things," *Rebbe* Doresh commented. "I've noticed that every time she comes here, she tries to push it. 'Car-car,' she calls it. I just hope she'll like shopping carts just as much when she's older and Mrs. Sheinbaum asks her to go shopping for her!"

Rebbe Doresh laughed, and the rest of the family did, too.

"I'm sorry I accused you of losing my dictionary, Chaim," Devora said softly.

"Oh, that's okay," Chaim replied generously. "We've solved two mysteries today—the case of the stolen dog and the case of the misplaced dictionaries."

"And the two mysteries also taught you an important lesson," Mrs. Doresh added. "Be slow to make accusations. *Don l'kaf z'chus*—that's the Jewish way."

The Haunted Shul

he air-conditioned bus moved quickly, almost noiselessly along the highway. It was a warm day and most of the passengers had dozed off. The only sound in the coach was Hasidic music from a harmonica and a *halil* in the back. Devora Doresh and Shaindy Nussbaum were traveling with their friend, Elisheva Gross, to the small town in the Catskill Mountains where Elisheva's mother lived. Elisheva stayed at the dormitory of the Yocheved High School all year long, but once each month she made the trip home to spend a weekend with her mother. Her father had died two years before. Since then Elisheva and her three brothers, who were also in New York studying at various yeshivoth, had arranged that each of them should go home for another weekend so Mrs. Gross would never be alone for Shabbos. "My wonderful kids," Mrs. Gross would tell her friends.

"I'm glad the school didn't plan a Lag B'Omer trip for this year," Shaindy said, taking her harmonica from her lips. "Yes," said Devora, "everybody decided they had something else important to do—weddings, concerts, family get-togethers. It was a good idea of Rabbi Margulies not to have the trip but to give us a long weekend off instead. Just think—from Thursday to Monday! Perfect!"

"And that makes it great for me," said Elisheva, putting down her *halil*. "This way I was able to invite you girls for Shabbos. It's fun to have some company on the bus."

"Tell me, Elisheva," Shaindy began. "Isn't your mother ever going to move? Living in the Catskills may be beautiful, but it's so far away from everything and everybody. Why does your mother still live there?"

Elisheva's eyes clouded over for a moment. "She has to sell the business and the house," Elisheva replied sadly. Then she brightened a little. "Once that's over, I'll become a regular New Yorker from Brooklyn."

"Rah! Rah! A Brooklynite," Shaindy shouted and drew a long breath on her harmonica.

Just then a man from the front of the bus walked toward them. He looked tired.

"Excuse me, young ladies," he said to the three girls. "But I have a terrible headache, and the long ride isn't helping it much. If you could just be a little quieter . . ."

"Of course," Devora said. "We hope our music didn't cause your headache."

The man smiled, then sighed. "With those beautiful *niggunim** you were playing? No indeed! I always enjoy listening to Hebrew songs. But I've been traveling almost twelve hours without a stop and I'm tired."

"Twelve hours! Wow!" Shaindy exclaimed. "Where are you from?"

*Spiritual melodies

Devora shook her head. "Really, Shaindy! I don't think it's any of our business."

The stranger smiled again. "Oh, that's all right," he said. "I've just arrived from Europe. And you really do play that harmonica quite nicely."

Shaindy was pleased. "I've been taking lessons in harmonica, and in piano, too," she said. "Do you play any instruments?"

"I play the violin. When I was a boy, my mother hoped I would become a concert violinist. I practiced for hours every day, but I never made it."

"What do you do, Mr.—?" Elisheva asked.

"My name's Perlman," the stranger replied. "I work for museums. I check paintings to see whether they're authentic or fakes."

Devora pursed her lips. "Do you happen to know about those paintings that have been disappearing from museums in Europe? I've been reading about them in the newspapers."

"I know something about them," Mr. Perlman said.

"What's this all about?" asked Shaindy.

"During the past year a number of paintings have been stolen from museums in Europe," Devora explained. "There is suspicion that whoever stole them smuggled them out of Europe and brought them here to the United States. But of course that's merely conjecture. There are no suspects."

Mr. Perlman nodded again. "You seem to be quite up to date on crime, young lady," he laughed.

"Are you kidding?" Shaindy asked. "Devora is our mystery solver. Nothing stops that kid."

Mr. Perlman chuckled. "I'll remember that in case I ever need any help."

Suddenly, the bus slowed down and veered into another lane of the highway.

"What's going on?" asked Elisheva.

"There must be some construction work up ahead," said Devora.

There was a long line of cars ahead of the bus, creeping along at a snail's pace. The girls sat back in their seats and looked out of the wide bus windows.

"We're almost home anyway," said Elisheva. "I can see the *shul* on top of the hill over there."

"What *shul?*" asked Shaindy.

"The haunted *shul.*"

"A haunted *shul?*" Mr. Perlman asked in surprise.

"That's another mystery I wouldn't mind having Devora solve," said Elisheva. "We have a haunted *shul* in our town."

The bus stopped. A policeman signalled the cars from the other lane to move first. But the girls did not notice. They were staring at the house high on top of the hill to the left.

"It reminds me of the house of Seven Gables," Mr. Perlman said.

"You know, it does look haunted," said Shaindy with just a hint of fear in her eyes.

"How long has it been haunted?" Devora asked.

"It started just before Passover," Elisheva replied.

"That's about five weeks!" Shaindy exclaimed. "This place is beginning to give me the creeps."

"So tell us, Elisheva," Devora demanded. "What makes it haunted?"

"The *shul* cries. Every night. Some nights, it literally wails," Elisheva began.

"Please," Devora pleaded. "Let's start the story from the beginning."

"Okay, here goes," said Elisheva. "That house didn't start out as a *shul*. It belongs to a man from Mexico who had it designed and built especially for himself. This happened long before we moved here. I don't remember whether Senor Carlos had the house brought over from Mexico brick by brick, or whatever, but I know that he lived there all by himself. Senor Carlos, you see, is a *very* wealthy man. Even Mr. Patell, who's a millionaire, envies him for that house. Everybody says that Mr. Patell spends months each year traveling through Europe to find a house like Senor Carlos' house which he could move here. But he hasn't found such a place yet."

"This Senor Carlos of yours," Mr. Perlman asked, "is Carlos his last name or his first?"

"It's his first name," Elisheva replied. "I could never pronounce his last name. So we always just called him Senor Carlos. He liked my mother and felt sorry for her when my father passed away. He loves music, just like my mother. Many years ago, he taught her to play the harp."

"The harp? I don't know anybody who plays *that*," said Shaindy.

"Well, my mother plays it beautifully," said Elisheva proudly.

"So Senor Carlos lives in that house all by himself?" Devora inquired.

"No more," Elisheva replied. "About half a year ago he suddenly told everybody he was leaving for Spain. Then from Spain, he sent word to his lawyer that he wanted to donate his house to be converted into a new Orthodox *shul* for our town."

"You mean Senor Carlos is Jewish, and a religious man?"

"Well, nobody thought he was. And Mr. Patell was quite upset. He'd wanted to buy the house and live in it himself. That's when Mr. Carlos' lawyer told him he couldn't buy it because Mr. Carlos wanted it to be turned into a *shul*."

"Wow!" said Shaindy. "I bet Mr. Patell offered a lot of money for that house."

"He did," Elisheva continued. "He told the lawyer he'd be willing to pay plenty for the house—enough for Senor Carlos to be able to build a magnificent modern *shul* for the Orthodox community. But Senor Carlos wouldn't hear of it."

"How did the people in the town feel about that?" Mr. Perlman asked.

"The town was split right down the middle," Elisheva answered. "Some felt that the house was so beautiful and distinguished that it would make a most unusual *shul*. Others said it would be better to take Mr. Patell's money, fix up our old *shul* and give the rest of the money to charity."

"Well, I guess there are always two sides to every question," said Devora with a smile.

"In the end, the people who wanted to keep Senor Carlos's house as a *shul* won out," Elisheva continued. "The needed alterations were begun, and an open house was supposed to be held a week before Passover. The afternoon before, a very generous gift arrived from Mr. Patell—a beautiful Star of David to be set as an ornament into the north tower of the *shul*. The star is beautiful, but also a little unusual. You see, it is constructed from six silver flutes. It's not all that big, but the silver certainly is bright. You can see it even from here!" She pointed to the hill. The sun beamed on the silver star. "It's blinding to look up there!" Devora exclaimed.

"Look! Now we have the answer to why our bus slowed down!" Shaindy cried. There had been an accident, which had blocked the two other lanes of the highway.

"The driver must have been blinded by the sunlight reflected by that Star of David and moved into the wrong lane," Elisheva said. "I tell you, it's hard to believe how much trouble that *shul* has been causing in our town."

"Trouble? Why?" Mr. Perlman inquired.

"Well, only a few hours before the open house, the carpenter was installing the Star of David into the tower. But then there must have been an unusually strong gust of wind. He fell off his ladder and broke both his arms. And that wasn't all. At the dinner, Mrs. Miller, the wife of the president, got a fish bone stuck in her throat and had to be rushed to the hospital. Then, the rabbi who was supposed to speak suddenly got a call to come to Brooklyn immediately. His son at yeshiva suddenly got very sick. So—a spoiled dinner and no speech."

Devora shook her head. "All this is horrible. But does that make the shul haunted?"

"Yes, it does. Because that night we heard the *shul* crying," Elisheva replied.

"Who's 'we'?" Devora demanded.

"Me, my mother, and a couple of other members of the *shul*. We'd all gone back later in the evening to make sure that everything from the open house had been cleaned up and put away. That's when we heard it for the first time."

"Did anybody ever investigate where the crying might come from?" Devora asked.

"Mr. Patell brought in somebody from Boston. The man was really quite nice about the whole thing. He stayed two nights and then he announced that there must be ghosts in the house just like in some of the old mansions in New England."

"Ghosts?" Shaindy demanded. "You must be joking, Elisheva."

"No, it's true," Elisheva insisted. "Jerry Long was riding his bike past the *shul* one night and he claims he actually saw the ghosts."

"Really?" Shaindy asked. "So how many did he see? What did they look like?"

"It isn't funny, Shaindy." said Elisheva. "Jerry is a law student and a very serious guy. He said he heard noises coming from the house, so he decided to ride up and see what was going on. It was a dark night—no moon. And he *saw* the ghosts. They scared the daylights out of him, too."

"And that's all? What happened then?" Devora asked.

"Mr. Patell suggested that we forget about using the house as a *shul*. 'Just leave it alone,' he said. He didn't want it for himself anymore, either. But he felt so sorry for our congregation that he offered to donate some money for us to fix up our old *shul*. Mr. Patell is a very nice man."

Devora looked at Mr. Perlman and frowned. "This Mr. Patell seems too nice to be for real. I don't think you ought to trust him."

"You may even have a chance to meet him, Devora," Elisheva went on. "We're having a campfire on the grounds of the old *shul* Saturday night, after Shabbos. Mr. Patell often joins us at our campfires and tells us all about his travels. He just spent a couple of weeks in Europe again."

Mr. Perlman looked closely at Devora. "I read about him in the papers. He returned to this country only yesterday. Mr. Patell is a well-known traveler."

"And so, it seems, is Mr. Perlman," Devora thought. But she said nothing.

The bus had started to move again and was gathering speed.

"Just a few more minutes and we'll be there" Elisheva announced happily.

The bus pulled up at the station shed. "Look!

There's my mother!" Elisheva exclaimed upon disembarking, waving at the same time to a pretty woman standing next to an old car. Mrs. Gross hugged her daughter and gave the other two girls a friendly welcoming smile. "I'm so glad to meet my daughter's friends," she said.

"I had a most interesting talk with these three young ladies," Mr. Perlman said. Elisheva introduced him to her mother.

"Where are you staying, Mr. Perlman?" Mrs. Gross asked.

"Oh, I've reserved a room in town," Mr. Perlman replied.

"But what'll you do for Shabbos? What about food?"

Mr. Perlman smiled. "Don't worry about me, Mrs. Gross. I brought some kosher food with me. I need this Shabbos for a good rest."

"What brings you to our town?" Mrs. Gross inquired.

"For the next couple of days I hope to do some painting," Mr. Perlman answered, "and perhaps even practice on my violin."

Devora laughed. "What a coincidence! Sherlock Holmes also played the violin."

Mrs. Gross looked questioningly at Devora, then at her daughter. The girls said good-by to Mr. Perlman and piled into Mrs. Gross' car.

That evening, Mrs. Gross played the harp for her daughter's guests. She had not played in many years, but it was beautiful.

"You know, Mrs. Gross," said Devorah, "when I hear you play the harp it makes me think of a story *Morah* Hartman told us at Yocheved High. King David had a harp suspended over his bed. At midnight, a north wind would pass between its strings and make the harp play. When David heard the music he would get up and study the Law. And when the people heard the chant of their king as he studied the Torah, they said, 'If our king can take time out from his many tasks to study the Torah, then we, who have much less to do, should certainly study also.' Anyway, Mrs. Gross, your music is beautiful and it's made me very happy."

Mrs. Gross had tears in her eyes. "Thank you, dear. You're very kind," she said softly.

The next day, Friday morning, Elisheva took her two friends for a walk around the town. Devora bought herself a flashlight at the general store. "I never go to a campfire without a flashlight," she explained. "I want to be able to see after the fire's gone out."

They passed the town hall. To their surprise, they saw Mr. Perlman come out from the side entrance.

"What are you doing here?" Shaindy asked inquisitively.

Mr. Perlman smiled. "I find this town a very interesting place," he said, then walked away without another word.

"He's a funny guy," Elisheva commented.

"Yes," said Devora. "But I think he's an honest man."

"How can you say he's honest when you hardly know him, Devora?" Elisheva demanded. "And then you say that you don't trust Mr. Patell, whom you've never even met?"

Devora shrugged her shoulders. "That's just the way I feel," she muttered, unable to explain just why she felt that way.

Friday night, after supper, the girls took another walk. Elisheva showed them the old *shul*. "Tomorrow night we'll have our campfire in the back of this *shul*," she told her friends.

"But when can we visit the other—I mean the haunted *shul*?" Devora asked.

"I'm not exactly crazy about the idea," said Elisheva. "There's something scary about the whole place. I understand all kinds of animals go prowling around there at night."

"And the *shul* cries only at night, I assume?" Devora inquired, with a little smile.

"Yes," said Elisheva. "And it's not what you think, either. It's not the animals that cry at night. It really is the *shul*."

Devora smirked. "And how do you know that it's not the ghosts who're crying?"

"It's easy for you to laugh," Elisheva pouted. "But you're my guests and I don't want to have anything happen to you. So, please, don't let's go there when it's dark."

Devora sighed. Here was a mystery ready-made for her, but it seemed that she would never have a chance to find out more about it.

Shabbos started out as a beautiful day, but later the sky became cloudy.

"Oh, I hope it won't rain," said Shaindy. "I *would* like a campfire."

"Here in the mountains it can be very cloudy without any rain at all, or it could rain for just a few minutes and then turn beautiful," Elisheva said. "You'll have your campfire yet."

By the time Shabbos had ended, it had not rained. The girls got ready to go to the campfire. Devora took along her new flashlight. On the way to the old *shul,* they met Mr. Perlman.

"Well, how are you girls doing?" he asked.

Elisheva smiled. "We're going to the campfire. Would you like to join us? You might even meet Mr. Patell. I'm sure he could tell you some interesting stories about our town."

"Thank you very much for your invitation, young lady," Mr. Perlman said. "But I rented a car and I just want to drive around the place a little."

When the girls arrived at the campfire site, some of Elisheva's friends were already there, and soon Elisheva was busy talking with them and building the fire. "I hope it won't rain tonight," said one of the girls looking up at the dark sky.

"If it didn't rain all day, why should it start now?" another girl said.

A tall, thin man had joined the group. "That's Mr. Patell," Elisheva whispered to Devora.

"Well, where did you go this time, Mr. Patell?" asked one girl.

"I was in Spain, hoping to run across Senor Carlos," Mr. Patell replied. "But I had no luck. From Spain, I went to Morocco. Now that's a place to visit."

"And did you take your flutes with you?" the girl asked.

"He has quite an unusual collection of flutes," Elisheva whispered to Devora. "The silver flutes that make up the Star of David in the haunted *shul* were part of that collection."

"Well, I didn't take all my instruments with me," Mr. Patell was saying. "But I took my oboe. This oboe goes with me wherever I travel. It means a lot to me. The man who gave it to me was a very special person." He went to his car and returned moments later to the campfire with the long, thin musical instrument.

"Do you actually play the oboe, Mr. Patell?" Devora asked.

Elisheva had taken out her *halil* and began to play it.

"Not as well as that girl over there plays her recorder," Mr. Patell replied. He looked at his wristwatch and turned to leave. But first he produced a bag of little gifts—colorful jewelry, leather wallets and silk scarves—which he gave out to the girls.

"Souvenirs," Elisheva explained. "He always does that when he comes back from a trip."

"He seems to have plenty of money to spend," Devora remarked.

"Like I told you, he's a nice man," said Elisheva.

After Mr. Patell had left, the girls examined their gifts, giggling and talking. But when they were ready to cook their hot dogs, it got chilly. Elisheva looked worried. "It looks like it's going to rain after all . . ." she said, and at that moment the skies opened. The heavy rain put out the fire almost at once. Then came thunder and flashes of lightning. The girls ran to the *shul* door, but it was locked.

"We'll try and make it home," said a few of the girls, running in the pelting rain.

"Let's wait a while," others said. "It might stop in a few minutes."

But the rain did not stop. Finally, Elisheva said, "I guess we'd better go home."

"Is there a shortcut?" Devora asked. She was soaking wet and shivering.

"Sure," said Elisheva, running toward a cluster of trees. "Come this way!"

Elisheva, Shaindy and Devora ran into the woods as the rain poured down in torrents. The thunder and lightning never stopped.

"This is crazy and dangerous," Devora shouted above the roar of the thunder. "We could get killed! You're not supposed to be outdoors in a storm like this, especially not in the woods."

That was when they heard the long, loud wail. Shaindy stopped in her tracks, terrified. "What's that?" she gasped.

"That's the haunted *shul,* crying again!" Elisheva yelled back.

"Isn't there some kind of shelter near here?" Devora asked.

"Just the haunted *shul,*" Elisheva replied.

A flash of lightning lit up the sky and Devora could see the strange-looking house in a clearing about 100 feet away.

"The haunted *shul!*" she shouted. "Let's get inside."

"No!" Elisheva cried, shivering with fear. "I'm not going in there!"

Suddenly there was a loud crash—not far behind them.

"Good G-d!" Elisheva cried. "One of the trees must have been struck by lightning!"

"Well, it just missed us," said Devora. "I don't know what you girls want to do, but I'm willing to take my chances. I think it's more dangerous to be outdoors than inside the haunted *shul.*"

Devora ran toward the shul. She pointed to a basement window from which the glass pane was missing. "We'll stay inside right next to that window," she suggested. "So if anything happens, we can get out fast." She climbed through the window. Shaindy and Elisheva followed reluctantly. At least they were in a dry place.

"I had a bad cold last week," said Shaindy, shivering, "and I finally got rid of it. I hope I won't come down with pneumonia from this."

Devora took out her flashlight, turned it on and flashed it around the room. There was a pile of sheets and rags on the floor. "Look girls! We could use those rags as towels or blankets." She picked up one of the sheets. It was not too dirty. "Come on, Shaindy! Throw this around your shoulders!"

"But my clothes are soaked!" Shaindy protested.

"Here's another sheet. Try to dry yourself with it," said Devora.

Elisheva stayed near the window. She stood quite

still and stared into the night. Time and again there it was, the long, drawn-out wail. And whenever it came, Elisheva turned to the others, her eyes darting around the room.

Devora, however, could not stand still. She had noticed a door on the other side of the room. She tip-toed over to it and carefully turned the knob.

"Where are you going?" Shaindy whispered. "You can't leave us alone here!"

The door creaked open and Devora shined her flash-light into the dark space. "Look!" she shouted, pointing to something inside the next room.

Shaindy was behind her almost instantly. Elisheva hung behind, but then her curiosity got the better of her and she followed the others. She did not want to miss anything.

The three girls followed the beam from Devora's flashlight to a table in the center of the room. Lying flat on the table was a beautiful painting of a ship out at sea, its sails puffing out in the wind. The waves lapped gently at the ship, and there was a captain, too, waving farewell to a lone woman standing on the shore.

Devora looked around the room, shining her flash-light in every direction. The beam picked out a heavy picture frame standing on the floor, resting against the wall. "You know, that frame must belong to the paint-ing." Devora bent and touched the frame. "Now I wonder: why isn't the painting in its frame?"

"It must have curled," said Shaindy. "Look." There was a small marble weight at each corner of the paint-ing. "Whoever this painting belongs to probably wanted to straighten out the edges. So he removed the painting from the frame and put on these weights."

There was a loud clap of thunder. Elisheva shuddered and ran back to the basement window. "Let's get out of here!" she pleaded with Devora. "I'm scared!"

"Listen! Somebody's moving upstairs!" cried Shaindy. The girls looked up to the ceiling. "There's somebody in this house," Devora whispered.

"The ghosts!" Elisheva shouted, and climbed out the basement window. Shaindy was right behind her. Devora hesitated at first, but then she followed the two other girls.

The rain was still coming down as the three girls ran back toward the woods. Elisheva turned around to make sure that her friends were behind her. Again, there was a flash of lightning. Elisheva's face was white. "The ghosts! There they are!" she whispered, pointing at the haunted *shul* behind them. Shaindy and Devora both turned around. They, too, saw a white figure moving near the window of the house. Elisheva did not look where she was walking. She lost her footing and fell heavily to the ground.

"Are you all right, Elisheva?" Devora asked.

Elisheva could only moan. "Oh! My ankle!" She rubbed her right foot.

Shaindy pointed to a mudhole. "You must have stepped into that," she said. Elisheva tried to get up but fell again. She moaned, and the wail from the haunted *shul* joined in. She began to cry.

"There must be a highway somewhere near here, so

we could stop a car for help," said Devora. "But just where is it?"

Elisheva pointed to the left.

Devora took off her scarf and tied it tightly around Elisheva's ankle. Then she and Shaindy helped Elisheva to her feet. "Could you hop on your left leg as far as the highway?" Shaindy asked. "We'll hold you."

"I'll try," Elisheva moaned. "But please go slow."

The girls were lucky. Just as they reached the highway, they were almost blinded by the headlights of a car. Devora waved her flashlight to stop the driver. The car came to a stop, and the driver opened the door. It was Mr. Perlman.

"Well, well," said Mr. Perlman. "One certainly picks up odd strangers in the country when it rains. Want a ride?" His amused look changed to concern when he saw Elisheva's white face and noticed that she was barely able to stand although her friends were holding her. He got out of the car and helped Elisheva in, then looked at her ankle. "Doesn't look too good," he said, shaking his head. "I think we should go to the hospital to have it X-rayed." Already, Elisheva's ankle had begun to swell.

Shaindy and Devora climbed into the car. "I hope that ankle isn't broken," said Mr. Perlman.

"The hospital is at the other end of town," Elisheva volunteered.

"We'll get you to the hospital and call your parents from there," Mr. Perlman said as he started the car. "Where were you girls anyway, in this rain?"

"Inside the *shul*," Shaindy croaked.

"Oh, I know, you had your campfire."

"Yes, but we couldn't get into that *shul*. We were inside the haunted *shul*."

Mr. Perlman laughed a little. "Did you see any ghosts?"

"Yes, we certainly did," said Elisheva and Shaindy.

Mr. Perlman looked straight ahead at the highway as the rain fell faster and heavier on the windshield. "Just what were your ghosts doing?" he asked.

"Well. . . . We only saw one, after we left," said Devora hesitantly.

"There was a room with a beautiful painting on a table," Shaindy cut in.

"What kind of painting?" Mr. Perlman asked. Elisheva began to describe it but suddenly she stopped and shouted, "Turn left!" There was the township hospital with its welcoming lights. Mr. Perlman drove up to the emergency entrance. An orderly came out and helped Elisheva from the car into a wheelchair. "You just wait here," he told the others. "I'll take her to the examining room."

"We'd better call Elisheva's mother," Shaindy said. One of the nurses directed Shaindy to a public telephone and she placed the call.

"I've been sitting by the phone all evening," Mrs. Gross told her. "I was worried about you girls. I'll get my car out right away and drive to the hospital."

Meanwhile Mr. Perlman was going through his wallet. He pulled out a snapshot and handed it to Devora. "Is this by any chance the painting you saw?" he asked.

Devora gasped. "Yes, Mr. Perlman. It is."

"So my information is correct," said Mr. Perlman. "The stolen paintings end up here, in this country."

"And who would bring them here?" Then, Devora understood. "You mean Mr. Patell, the well-known traveler?"

"That's what it looks like, Devora. As soon as we know how Elisheva is we'll have to go back to the *shul* and look at that painting."

A half hour late Mrs. Gross walked into the hospital lobby with Mrs. Koenig, a friend. "Mr. Perlman, I must thank you for finding the girls," she said.

"It was my pleasure," he replied.

Mrs. Gross headed for the examining room. A doctor was just coming from that direction. "I suppose you are Mrs. Gross," he said.

"Yes," said Mrs. Gross. "How's my daughter? Is her foot—"

"I'm afraid she does have a broken ankle, Mrs. Gross. But it's not a bad break. We're just putting on the cast. You'll be able to take her home later."

"I see that everything's under control, Mrs. Gross," Mr. Perlman said. "I think Devora and I still have some business to do."

"So late at night?" Mrs. Gross smiled. She was relieved that her daughter was not badly hurt.

"Don't worry, Mrs. Gross. We won't be long. I'll bring Devora back safely to your house."

"You're not really going back to that haunted *shul* without *us*," said Shaindy. Devorah looked at Mrs. Koenig and Shaindy. They would go too.

In the car, Mr. Perlman told Devora more about his work.

"I'm an investigator for museums. I investigate forgeries and thefts from exhibits. When this particular painting was stolen, I got clues which led to this town. Lately, whenever a painting was stolen from one of the museums in Europe, Mr. Patell just happened to be visiting there. The question now remaining is how he does each job, and what he does with the paintings once he has them in this country."

When they got to the haunted *shul,* the rain had stopped and the wind had died down. Devora showed Mr. Perlman the basement window through which she and the other girls had climbed in. Then she led everyone inside to the door and the room behind it.

"The painting! It's gone!" Devora exclaimed. The frame was gone, too. Only the marble weights were still on the table. "Somebody must have come in here after we left!"

"The ghosts?" Mrs. Koenig raised a questioning eye.

There it was again, the long, unearthly wail. "The *shul's* crying again!" Devora exclaimed. "Let's go upstairs. Let's hurry." They climbed the stairs and walked through each of the rooms on the upper floor. The rooms were empty. Finally, they reached the tower where the silver Star of David had been installed. They looked out of the window at the woods below.

"This *is* a scary place," Mr. Perlman admitted. They went down the steps again, back to the basement.

Devora felt tired and hot. She wanted to wipe her

forehead. She remembered the rags and sheets she and her friends had seen piled up on the floor. Where were they now? She looked for the sheets, but they were gone; like the painting and the frame, they seemed to have vanished into thin air.

Back in the car, Devora was very quiet.

"A penny for your thoughts," said Mr. Perlman.

"I have to sort them out. They're all mixed up."

"Well, in that case, young lady, go right ahead and think out loud. I'd like to hear your mixed-up thoughts."

"Okay, Mr. Perlman. The painting which we saw was the one you have a picture of. So it's obviously the stolen painting you've been looking for. When the girls and I were in the basement of the *shul*, waiting for the rain to stop, we heard footsteps from the floor above. That must have been the people who stole the painting. The thieves must have taken the painting out of its frame, left the frame behind and rolled the painting up to get it out of the museum without anybody noticing that something was wrong. During the trip from Europe, the painting got curled up, so it had to be straightened. That was the reason for the weights on the table. The thieves bought a new frame here, into which they were going to put the painting as soon as it was straightened out. The thieves came to the *shul* to reframe the painting and to get it out of the house. But then the heavy rain started. . . . Mr. Perlman, do you think we could go back and have another look around the place? You see, when we were in the basement, we saw a heap of sheets and rags on the floor, but now they have disappeared. I think the painting must still be somewhere in the house, except that now it'll be in the new frame and covered with the sheets, ready to be taken out."

Mr. Perlman nodded and drove back to the *shul.* They all went through the rooms again, but could see no sign of the painting.

"So what do we do now?" Shaindy gestured hopelessly. "I give up."

"Well, this house is a very strange place. There may be little rooms and corners we wouldn't find in a million years. So, we'll just have to let the thieves show us the way," Devora replied.

"How do we do that?" Mr. Perlman was impressed.

"I'm thinking of a legend we learned in school the other day. Our teacher is great on legends. It seems that a storekeeper was robbed and came to the rabbi of his town for help in finding the thief. The rabbi called a meeting of all the people living in the town. Then he ordered his assistant to take the door of the store from its hinges and bring it before the people. The door, he said, would have to stand trial and be punished for not having done its work, which was to keep intruders out. The rabbi ordered his assistant to give the door a whipping so it would tell who the theives were.

"After the door got its whipping, the rabbi put his ear close to the door, as if he were listening to someone talking. Then he stood up and said: 'The door told me that when the thief entered the store, a cobweb from the ceiling settled down on his head. So all we have to do now is look for a man who has a piece of cobweb on his head.' At that moment one of the men in the crowd of townspeople put his hand to his head. The rabbi pointed his finger at him. 'There we have our thief,' he said. 'You put your finger to your head; you wanted to remove the cobweb.' Of course it was all an act; the door never talked, and there never had been a cobweb, but the rabbi's little act tricked the thief into confessing. So now, Mr. Perlman, we also will have to invent a little act of our own to make our thief come out into the open."

"So what do you suggest we do, young lady?" Mr. Perlman asked.

"We have to get word around that a special detective is coming to investigate the haunted *shul*. When Mr. Patell gets wind of this, he will want to move the painting out of the *shul* quickly. So we will have to have someone stay around and watch for him."

Mr. Perlman looked at his watch. "A very smart idea," he said. "But now we have to get you to your friend's house before her mother wonders whether you've been kidnapped. It's way past midnight."

Early the next morning, Mr. Perlman stopped again at Elisheva's house. This time he brought a bunch of flowers for the patient, who was sitting in the living room in an easy-chair, her right leg encased in a plaster cast.

"How are you feeling, Elisheva?" he asked.

"Uncomfortable and miserable," Elisheva replied.

Mrs. Gross invited Mr. Perlman to stay for breakfast. "We're having pancakes," she said.

"It's hard to turn down a good home-cooked meal,"

Mr. Perlman replied. "But I'm afraid there are some important phone calls I have to make."

"That's all right, Mr. Perlman," said Mrs. Gross. "Go into the den. You can make all the calls you want, undisturbed."

When he emerged from the den some time later, Mr. Perlman was smiling. "Tonight, Devora, we ought to have our answer," he said.

"And will you also find out why the *shul* has been crying?" Shaindy asked.

"Maybe," Mr. Perlman replied, with a wink at Devora.

"Once we find out what's been causing all the screeching and wailing we might be able to get the *shul* ready in time for the holidays in the fall," said Mrs. Gross.

"Let's just keep it a secret between us until the mystery is solved," said Mr. Perlman. Then he changed the subject. "Who plays the harp in your family, Mrs. Gross? I saw a harp in the den."

"I used to play the harp a lot," Mrs. Gross replied. "But I haven't played it much since my husband died. . . ."

"I know what it's like, Mrs. Gross. I lost my wife many years ago. We had no children and I really felt lost. . . ."

Later, when Mr. Perlman left, Devora walked with him to the door.

"I don't think you'll be allowed to wait with me at the *shul* tonight," he said, "but I promise I'll call you the minute we catch the thieves."

After supper that evening, Devora and Shaindy packed their suitcases for the trip back to New York. Mrs. Gross had suggested that they not leave until early the next morning, because Devora was anxious to find out what had happened at the haunted *shul*.

Late in the evening, Mr. Perlman came again, fairly beaming. "Our hunch was correct. There was a room we missed in our search. And our man was Mr. Patell," he said. "Patell actually managed to steal about 14 paintings from museums and collections all over Europe. He was quite good at it, too. He had a special way of rolling up his paintings very tightly around a—"

"Now I understand," Devora eagerly exclaimed. "It was his oboe! He used his oboe as a stick around which to roll his paintings. The oboe which he said he took everywhere but never played."

Mr. Perlman nodded. "When he brought the stolen paintings here, he needed a place to straighten them out and to re-frame them. He found that Senor Carlos' house—your haunted *shul*—was the perfect place for such operations. Its walls are thick so that there's no humidity, ever. Also, the place is slightly off the beaten track. That's why Mr. Patell was so anxious to buy the house and have it all to himself. But he wanted to make sure, also, that strangers would keep away from the place. So he made up the story about the house being haunted. He's no dummy, that Mr. Patell."

"True," Devora agreed and added, "and the flutes that make up the Star of David have holes in them, of course, for the music. And he knew that you have some good strong north winds here. That's how the carpenter got to fall off his ladder when he installed the Star of David. Well, whenever the north wind comes it blows through the holes of the flute and makes that weird music. It sounds like weeping and wailing—loud enough to scare people off. Now, if the congregation wants to stop the crying from the *shul,* all you need to do is plug up the holes in the flute. Then the *shul* won't be haunted anymore."

"But what about the ghosts?" asked Shaindy.

"That's right," said Elisheva. "We *saw* the ghosts and so did Jerry!"

Devora nodded her head and smiled. "Well," she said, "it really wasn't a ghost we saw. Do you remember the pile of sheets on the basement floor? After the painting was unrolled and straightened in the basement, Mr. Patell replaced them in their frame. Then he carried the painting, covered by the white sheets, up the stairs to the main floor and outside to the waiting car. Don't you remember," she turned to Shaindy, "before we fled from the *shul* you said that you heard somebody moving around upstairs!"

Shaindy clapped her hands as she remembered the incident. "You mean the ghost was just the white sheet covering the painting as Mr. Patell passed the stairway window?"

Devora grinned. "The white sheet reflected the flashes of lightning. My guess is that Jerry must have seen the same 'ghost' we saw. And, of course, people become susceptible to suggestion with the eerie sound of wailing on dark nights in deserted areas."

Mrs. Gross heaved a sigh of relief. "I'm glad that this

mystery is cleared up," she said. "I know Senor Carlos will be glad to hear about it, too. He's coming back for the holidays in the fall. A letter came from him yesterday." She turned to Elisheva who was resting on the couch. "In all the excitement, I haven't even told you yet, Elisheva. Senor Carlos is interested in buying our house. And he says he wants to see whether he can't find someone to buy your father's business. Then we could move to New York and live in Brooklyn. I have some good friends there, and it appears that you have friends there also."

"What an interesting coincidence," said Mr. Perlman. "Brooklyn is my home base, too. I wouldn't mind working from the United States, for a change, and let Europe get along without me. If you really move back to Brooklyn, I'd be glad to help you settle down."

Just then, the strange sound came again from the *shul.* But this time, somehow, it sounded not like a wail but more like a high-pitched giggle.

Acknowledgements

I am grateful to many people without whose assistance this book would still be only a dream.

I owe a debt of gratitude to Ms. Gertrude Hirshler for her constructive criticism and editing of the manuscript.

The practical editorial contribution of Ms. Bonnie Goldman as well as the efforts of Ms. Devorah Kramer, who responded artistically with talented illustrations, deserve my warm and sincere thanks.

Particularly, I wish to express my gratitude to Mr. Jack Goldman of Judaica Press whose faith and invaluable guidance assured the completion of this book.

Finally, feelings of gratitude which cannot be put into words, must go for my husband who encouraged me with patience, dedication and good humor.

C.K.H.

About the Author

Carol Korb Hubner, daughter of the late Rabbi Moshe Korb and Mrs. Devora (Korb) Gartenberg, was born and raised in Chicago, Ill. until her early teens when she moved to Brooklyn with her family. She pursued her higher education at Stern College for Women where she received her B.A.

Mrs. Hubner has been a member of the presidium of the National Council of Bnos Agudath Israel and editor of its weekly newsletter. As counselor and head counselor of Camp Bnos her reputation as a story teller became legendary.

Wife to Rabbi Ehud Hubner, who is involved in scholarly talmudic research, mother of four children, and Bais Yaacov teacher, Mrs. Hubner's avocation is writing stories for young adults.